Angeline

Karleen Bradford

Angeline

HarperTrophyCanada™
An imprint of HarperCollins*PublishersLtd*

Published by Harper*Trophy*Canada™, an imprint of HarperCollins Publishers Ltd

Originally published in trade paperback: 2004

This mass market paperback edition: 2005

Harper*Trophy*Canada™ is a trademark of HarperCollins Publishers

HarperCollins books may be purchased for educational, business, or sales promotional use through our Special Markets Department.

HarperCollins Publishers Ltd
2 Bloor Street East, 20th Floor
Toronto, Ontario, Canada
M4W 1A8

www.harpercollins.ca

Library and Archives Canada Cataloguing in Publication

Bradford, Karleen
Angeline / Karleen Bradford. – 2nd ed.

ISBN-13: 978-0-00-639344-3
ISBN-10: 0-00-639344-6

1. Children's Crusade, 1212—Juvenile fiction. 2. Egypt—History—640-1250—Juvenile fiction. 3. Slavery—Juvenile fiction. 4. Belief and doubt—Juvenile fiction. I. Title.

PS8553.R217A76 2005 JC813'.54
C2005-902417-8

OPM 9 8 7 6 5 4 3 2

Printed and bound in the United States

For Emily and Paige

Prologue

In 1096 Pope Urban II of the Holy Roman Empire called for a holy war to recover Jerusalem from the Muslims, and reestablish the pilgrimage paths to the east. This resulted in a series of crusades which took place over the next two hundred years.

The first of these crusades began to assemble in the spring of that year. Before this army could make ready, however, a monk named Peter, unwilling to wait, left Cologne, Germany, on Easter weekend. He was followed by a ragtag band of pilgrims, thieves, and criminals who had been promised pardon if they went on crusade. This People's Crusade, as it is now called, ended in disaster when it was overwhelmed by the Muslim forces at Civetot, in Turkey. Most of those who had survived the arduous march across Europe were killed.

The army that the Pope had called for set out in September. In 1099, after almost three years of hardship and war, this first legitimate crusade succeeded in recapturing Jerusalem. The Christian kings of Jerusalem ruled for only eighty-eight years, however. In 1187 the great Muslim leader Salah-ud-Din, known to Christians as Saladin, retook the city.

A second crusade failed to reach Jerusalem. In 1192 a third crusade, led by King Richard Lionheart of England and King Philip of France, ended in a short-lived truce with Salah-ud-Din. A fourth crusade ended in disgrace with the sacking of Constantinople, a Christian city.

By the year 1212, the crusading fervour had waned. Then a shepherd boy, Stephen of Cloyes, had a vision in a field while tending his sheep. A man appeared to him, bearing a letter which he bade Stephen take to King Philip of France. It was a missive commanding Stephen to raise an army of children to march on Jerusalem. These children would accomplish what men had failed to do. By their faith alone, they would restore Jerusalem to Christendom. It was God's will, the mysterious stranger proclaimed.

Twenty thousand young people joined Stephen and marched across France to the seaside port of Marseilles. The journey was hard. Many of the children died of starvation or were murdered; many gave up in despair and tried to make their way home. Only about seven thousand survived to reach Marseilles. There, Stephen believed God would part the waters and he would lead them through to Jerusalem.

When the waters did not part, they set forth in ships that they were tricked into believing were to take them to the Holy Land. Two of these ships sank. The children in the remaining five ships were sold as slaves in the markets of North Africa and Egypt.

Chapter One

The sun beat down from a hard, blue, cloudless sky. Heat radiated back from the endless sand. There was no escape from it. Angeline stood on the stone block, swaying with dizziness. She managed one glance around her but couldn't face the crowd staring up at her. The man holding her shouted something and others shouted back. She knew not what they were saying, but she realized what they were doing—they were bargaining for her! She crossed her arms and hugged them close. Her face burned with shame. A slave. She was being sold as a slave.

She still could not make sense of it all. It had been such a glorious dream. Stephen's dream—and then hers.

She had first met Stephen on the road to her village market. She had been stumbling under the heavy load that her uncle—that cursed man—had forced her to carry. Stephen and the young priest who travelled with him, Father Martin, had been making their way along the same path. Stephen had offered to help, but her uncle had struck him with his stick, and railed at the priest when he sought to protect the boy.

"Begone with you, you black crow!" her uncle had shouted.

Her clodpole of an uncle. Angeline had had no love for priests—her own village priest, Father Bertrand, had hounded her mother to her death because she had not been properly wed and would tell no one who the father of her child was, but surely her uncle would go to hell for that blasphemy. She hoped he would.

The next morning in church after Mass, she had been surprised to see Father Bertrand thrust that same boy forward.

"My people. My flock," the priest had proclaimed in a triumphant voice. "You see before you a boy. Naught but a simple shepherd. Be not deceived by his poor appearance—this boy, Stephen, from the village of Cloyes, has been sent to us by God! He bears a letter that commands him to lead a crusade of innocents to the Holy Land. A letter which he has been bade to take to King Philip himself!"

He had turned to Stephen. For a long moment the boy had just stood there. Angeline thought that he looked terrified. Finally, he drew a deep breath and began to speak, but he could only stutter and his voice was so weak that some of the people laughed. She had felt a sudden surge of protectiveness toward him then. Surely he could not be much older than she, and she had seen but fourteen summers. How could a mere boy be summoned by God for such a mission?

But Stephen found his voice. He began to preach as if possessed by angels. Before her eyes he was transformed. He straightened and tossed back the lock of hair that fell into his eyes. His voice strengthened, became as powerful as Father Bertrand's—more powerful even. It rang out to fill every corner of the church. His whole body shuddered with the force that seemed to be pouring into him. There was no more laughter from the people. They sat open-mouthed and staring.

"This letter was given to me by the Christ Himself!" he announced. "It commands me to lead a new crusade to the Holy Land. To Jerusalem. To restore our sacred city to Christianity!"

Angeline had listened, amazed.

"Another crusade," he cried out. "Not, this time, a crusade of men armed with swords, but a crusade of the young such as ourselves," his eyes glowed with a fire that seemed to seek out and transfix every youth in the church. "Of children even, armed only with our faith! Follow me!" he cried. "Follow me and we will accomplish what men have failed to do. *We* will rescue Christendom itself!"

Angeline had heeded his call. It was a way to escape her uncle, but not only that. Stephen's words had awakened something within her. His dream had spoken to her and she wanted to be part of it . . .

A man's finger jabbed her in the ribs. She came back to the burning heat of the slave camp with a jolt and glared at him. She was not a beast to be treated so!

He shrugged, said a few words to the man who

held the rope that bound her wrists, then turned his back on her and walked away.

Was she not good enough for him then? She glared at his retreating back even more fiercely. She forced herself to keep her head high and stare haughtily at the crowd, but her stomach twisted with a cramp. It took all of her will to keep from being sick.

She could see the pen where she had spent the night. Many of the girls still remained there, pressed against the fence or slumped in despair. One in particular, Solange her name was, had not ceased crying since they had been dragged from the ship. Angeline had not wept since the night her mother had succumbed to the raging fever that took her life. That night, Angeline had wept until she could weep no more, alone and in the secrecy of her beloved forest. The next day, when Father Bertrand spoke his hypocritical words of comfort at her mother's burial, she had stood dry-eyed beside him. She refused even to acknowledge the fawning and false sympathy of the village women who had always disliked her mother, and who had joined the priest in censuring her. Of course, Angeline's dry eyes had only hardened them more to her.

"Not even a tear," one of them had whispered. It was she who had been quicker than any of the others to lay the sharp side of her tongue to Angeline whenever she could. "I always said she was a shameless little vixen."

The memory of that woman made Angeline raise her chin even higher. She willed herself to fan the flames of anger that burned within her. Only by feeding that rage, nourishing it, could she find the strength to fight the terror that threatened to overwhelm her. Keeping her eyes fixed above the heads of the crowd, Angeline stared at the harbour, where the ships that had brought them here rode at anchor, and to the sea beyond. The ruins of a great lighthouse stood guard on a point that jutted far out into the waters.

Somewhere across that sea was France. Somewhere across that vast expanse was the village that had been home to her all of her life. Until her mother had died. Until her uncle had arrived to take possession of her mother's meagre goods—and of Angeline herself. She stood as tall as she could, hands clenched into fists to keep them from shaking. But where were Stephen and Father Martin?

Stephen and Angeline had stood side by side as their ship had led the others into the harbour the day before. The children around them had cheered as the land drew nearer. Stephen had grasped Angeline's hand tightly.

"We have succeeded," he had said, his voice exultant.

Angeline had barely been able to hear him over the exuberant cries.

"The Holy Land!" He had bowed his head in prayer. Then he had turned to the captain of the ship.

"What arrangements have been made for our transport to Jerusalem?" he had asked. "How far is it?"

There were men standing near the plank that had been lowered to connect the ship with the land.

"Are those men here to guide us?" Stephen had asked. Angeline remembered how his voice had resumed its air of authority, but the captain had broken into jeering laughter.

"You really do not know what awaits you, my young simpleton, do you?" he said between guffaws. "You really believe this is the Holy Land! You are in Alexandria, my sorry lad. In Egypt. The land of the heathen and you are all to be sold as slaves."

Stephen had cried out in furious disbelief, but the slave traders had bounded up the plank and begun to round up the children, herding them roughly off the ship and onto the shore. The children's cries of joy changed to screams that Angeline could still hear echoing in her ears.

One of the slave traders grabbed Angeline and sought to pull her away. Stephen threw himself upon the man and beat at him with his fists.

"Leave her!" he had cried. "You will not touch her!"

Angeline struck out as well, but even as she did so another of the men smashed Stephen across the head with a staff. He fell to the deck, blood streaming from the wound.

"Stephen!" Angeline screamed and would have knelt to aid him, but she was seized yet again and dragged away. Stumbling, fighting with every bit of energy she possessed, she almost fell off the plank, then gasped as she was thrown down on the shore.

She and the other girls had been herded into pens. The boys and priests were taken to other enclosures. Try as she might, she had not been able to catch a glimpse of Stephen. She still did not know what had become of him. Did not know even if he lived. She had lain the past night in a stupor until the slave traders had reappeared this morning to haul her and the other girls off to the block to be sold.

Now she searched the swirling crowd around her for any sign of Stephen. She could see the pens where the boys were held, could even see another block at the other side of the enclosure where they were being sold, but she could catch no sight of Stephen. The men in the throng pressing in upon her were dark and bearded. They were dressed in long robes with coloured turbans wound around their heads. She saw donkeys, horses, and goats nosing around in whatever refuse they happened upon. There were huge, dun-coloured beasts there also. They had saddles of a sort upon their humped backs, but they were so tall she could not imagine how anyone could mount them. A few were lying down. She saw one animal spit what looked like a foul liquid into the sand upon which it lay. Evil-looking creatures, indeed. She shuddered.

There was no wind; the heat bore down in a smothering blanket. Flies and small biting insects swarmed around her, but with her hands bound she could not whisk them away. The sun shone with an unrelenting intensity. Huge dunes of sand surrounded the slave enclosures. Tall, fringe-leafed trees cast small pools of shade in which many of the men lolled. Some had built fires and were cooking food. The heat, the mingled smells of the food and the rank stink of the animals, the babbling of voices rising all around her, all of it was so overwhelming that she found herself gasping for air. Sweat poured into her eyes and drenched her shift.

Yet more men came and handled her. They grasped her under the chin with brutal fingers so that she was forced to look into their faces, smell their strong breath. One even pried her mouth open and looked at her teeth. Her mother had always encouraged her to clean them with twigs and herbs, and she knew they were in much better condition than those of other girls her age. She had not lost a single one and they never gave her pain. She had been proud of that, but now, as the man grunted with satisfaction, she wished she didn't have a tooth in her head. She fought back the impulse to bite him. He squeezed her arms to test for strength. After the hardships of the crusade she knew she was weak, but she was wiry even so. He nodded with satisfaction, obviously pleased that he would be able to get good work out of her. Then she cringed as she felt his hands on her shoulders. She had watched other girls being sold and she knew he was about to pull down her shift to inspect her body.

She heard a shout. Yet another man leaped up onto the block. This man was darker than any person she had ever seen; his skin shone deeply black in the sunlight. He held himself like a prince and his robes fell in rich, brilliantly hued folds around him. He barked out a word and to her astonishment the man who was inspecting her cowered and backed away. Then the black man narrowed his eyes and looked at her.

"Name?"

Angeline stared at him. He had spoken in French!

"Angeline," she answered.

He nodded and handed some coins to the man who held her rope. Her captor weighed them on a small scale, then let loose a volley of angry words. There followed a long and protracted exchange. Angeline's captor became ever more furious and voluble, but the black man bargained calmly. At one point he even took some of his coins back, causing an explosion of indignation. Finally, the sale was concluded. The rope was handed over to the black man and he motioned to Angeline to follow him.

"Viens," he commanded. *Come.*

Suddenly weak with fear in spite of her resolve, Angeline could barely summon the strength to step down off the block. What was to happen now? It was only with the greatest effort of will that she managed to stay on her feet and follow the man. He did not speak to her again, nor did he turn to see how she fared. She had to trot to keep up with his long strides. The crowd parted for him as he strode through it—he was obviously a man of some importance.

He led Angeline over to a grove of trees at the edge of all the hubbub. She could see three figures waiting there for him. Two of them were tethered to a stake and must also be slaves, she thought. One was taller than the other, dressed in a filthy black robe. Then, with a shock, she realized who they were. The robed man was Father Martin and the other—the other was Stephen! An ugly red welt on his forehead oozed blood, but he was alive.

"Stephen!" she cried and ran toward him.

Father Martin staggered forward and grasped her hands in his. He seemed stunned. Shocked. He tried to speak, failed, then managed to form words.

"Angeline," he gasped. "Thanks be to God you are found."

The priest's face was ashen. Angeline reached out to him. He took a deep breath, then spoke again.

"This man is called Zeid," he said. "He seems to be a good man." He caught his breath, then continued. "He bought me. He spoke French. We could talk. I implored him to find Stephen and purchase him as well, and he did so. Then, when he said he was to buy a slave girl, I entreated him to find you. I wanted to keep us together if I could. By God's will . . ." his voice trailed off.

Angeline stared at him. He it had been who had restored her confidence in priests. He it had been who had given them strength and helped keep their faith alive during all the desperate months of their journey. Not even when the children began to die had Father Martin's belief faltered.

"We are doing God's will," the priest had proclaimed, and preached it every morning when he and the other priests who had joined them said Mass. "We will set Jerusalem free!"

But he had been tricked just as thoroughly as they by the men who had promised them passage to the Holy Land. And now he looked beaten—as despairing as she.

Angeline's head was swimming. She would have pressed the priest further, but the man called Zeid interrupted her.

"There is no time for talk now," he said, still, to Angeline's wonder, in French. "We must set sail before the sun sinks any lower." He turned to a more poorly dressed man who seemed to be a servant, or perhaps another slave—she had no way of knowing—and said a few words she could not understand. The man untied Father Martin and Stephen from the stake, then took Angeline's rope as well.

Angeline turned again to Stephen, but he would not look at her. He swayed as he stood there, as pale as death.

"Stephen?" she whispered. "How fare you? What did they do to you?"

Finally, Stephen raised his eyes to meet hers,

but those eyes that had glowed with such fervour were blank and empty now. His voice was just as dead.

"What did they do to me?" he repeated. "No more than what they did to you and to all the others who survived to follow me here," he said. "They sold me. They have sold us *all* into hell."

Angeline could not suppress a muffled cry of protest. This could not be Stephen talking! She looked to Father Martin for help but he shook his head wordlessly. The servant tugged on their ropes. Zeid was already striding away from the slave market. They could do nothing but allow themselves to be led back to the shore. A small boat was tied up there, one white-robed man seated in the stern, his hand on the tiller, another at the bow.

Zeid untied their ropes.

"Get in," he ordered. In silence, they obeyed. He motioned them to take their places in the centre of the boat; the servant clambered into the stern. Zeid gave a command, and the boatmen pulled in the lines that connected them to the shore. They raised two sails and the boat came alive. It fairly leaped away from the land. They were once more at sea, tossing in the waves.

As they sailed out of the harbour, they passed under the prow of the vessel in which they had come. It looked strangely deserted, with its sails furled and oars shipped. Angeline could see no sign of the sailors, nor of the captain who had brought them here. He was in the cabin, no doubt, counting the coins he had received for them and gloating over the praise he would receive from the two treacherous swine who had promised Stephen and his followers safe passage from Marseilles to the Holy Land. William Porquierres and Hugo Ferrus. William the Pig and Hugo of Iron. Well named they were, indeed.

Stephen had had a vision from God that the waters of the sea would part for them at Marseilles, as they had for Moses. He had promised his followers that he would lead them safely to the Holy Land. But the waters did not part and Stephen's followers had been filled with fury. Many of them deserted him, those who remained were as despondent as he. And then those two wretched men had appeared. Stephen and Father Martin had welcomed them, certain that they had been sent by God. Angeline had not been so sure. She had distrusted them from the beginning, but she would not abandon Stephen. She felt the anger sweeping back at the memory and she welcomed it.

Now their small craft sailed along the coastline, then turned and made its way into the mouth of a great river whose waters ran brown and muddy into the sea. Once on the river the boat settled down and skimmed more smoothly over the surface. Only then did Zeid speak.

"You have all been purchased for the Emir, Abd'al Haseeb. I am his steward. He is a great prince, well-beloved and most trusted by our Sultan himself. He is a benevolent master and you will be well treated. The port where you landed was Alexandria. We go now to Cairo where Abd'al Haseeb lives. Cairo is a great city—the wonder of the world. You," he pointed to Father Martin, "you will be tutor to my master's eldest son, Habib. The Emir wishes the boy to become knowledgeable in the western languages. I can speak French, as you see, and have conversed with Habib in that language since he was a babe, but the Emir wishes him to learn to read and write Latin as well."

Father Martin drew himself up. Although Angeline could see his hands trembling, he managed to speak with defiance.

"You should know that I will not renounce my religion," he said. "I am a Christian priest, a servant of the one true God. I will die rather than betray my God."

"Be at ease," Zeid answered. "We who follow Islam are taught that you Christians and the Jews are Ahl al-Kitab, People of the Book. We respect Jesus as a great Prophet, as was Muhammad, peace be upon him. It is unfortunate that you Christians and the Jews have gone astray and left the true path, but we do not persecute you for your mistaken beliefs. We live together in our country in peace. The Jews pray in their temples, the Christians in their churches. You will be free to worship as you wish."

Father Martin looked disbelieving, but he clamped his lips shut and remained silent. Angeline was surprised. This was not what she had heard. Not what the priests had said when warning them about what would happen if they were captured.

"If you are seized you will be tortured," they had proclaimed. "You will be burned alive, slaughtered! Christian women will be dishonoured. The heathen hate our God. But hold fast to your faith and God will reward you in Heaven."

Angeline looked at Zeid. He looked back at her calmly. There was a peacefulness about him. Truly, this man was not what she had expected. But could he be trusted?

"The boy will assist you," Zeid went on, speaking once more to Father Martin. "And he will help in the gardens as well. We have need of another slave to help our gardener, Kareem. He is old and lacks someone young to work with him."

Angeline could hold her peace no longer.

"And me?" she asked. "What is to become of me?"

"You are to be slave to Zahra, the master's favourite concubine," Zeid replied. "You are fortunate."

Fortunate? Whatever a concubine was, how could she possibly be considered fortunate? They were supposed to have been the chosen children of God—the ones who would succeed where all others had failed. They were supposed to have been the ones who would march triumphant into Jerusalem and conquer the city by their faith alone. Theirs was to have been a destiny glorious beyond all comprehension.

Fortunate?

Angeline looked at Stephen, who sat crumpled beside her. He was staring at the brown waters swirling by. He seemed not to have heard anything of what Zeid had said. How could he be so indifferent? How could he not care what was to happen to them? To her? It was as if the boy she had come to admire and care for so deeply on their dreadful journey had disappeared. As if he had been replaced by a shell of a person. But she needed him! She was terrified! They were slaves in a strange, harsh land. Who knew what fate awaited them, despite the words of this man?

Chapter Two

Angeline sat in the boat and stared at the shore as it slipped by. Try as she might, she could not get Stephen to speak a word. She longed for him to talk to her. To reassure her. To chase away the pictures that flooded her mind no matter how hard she tried to block them out. Pictures of what might be awaiting them, each more frightening than the other.

"What is a concubine?" she asked Father Martin in a whisper.

He pursed his lips. "A woman who is like a

wife, but not a wife. Not wed. The heathen keep them as well as wives."

"They are allowed to do that?" Angeline asked incredulously. "No one disapproves?"

But Father Martin would say no more.

They pulled into the river shore just as the sun was setting. Angeline tensed. What would happen now? There was no sign of a city here or any dwellings at all. They could not have reached Cairo yet.

"We have gone as far as we can for today," Zeid announced. "You will not be tethered. There is nowhere to run should you try to escape. Come with me and I will show you."

Stephen sank down in a heap on the shore as the boatmen pulled the small craft up onto the bank and made it fast. He shook his head, wordlessly.

Angeline held back. She was not about to go anywhere alone with that man, no matter how civilized he seemed. She looked to Father Martin, unsure as to what she should do.

"I will come as well," the priest reassured her. He gave Stephen a worried glance, then turned to Zeid. "Stephen will stay here."

Zeid shrugged. "As you wish," he said.

Reluctantly, Angeline followed Zeid through the bushes that lined the riverbank. She made certain to keep Father Martin between her and the man. What was it he wanted to show them?

She cast a look back at Stephen, but he sat hunched into himself, staring at the river. He looked so desolate! She stopped—she could not just leave him there. She almost called out to urge him to come with them, then bit back the words. She looked at the marks on her wrists where the rope had burned. She could not help it—the anger that simmered within her turned now on him. It was because of *him* that she was here. It was because of *him* that she was a slave, doomed to a future far more horrible than any she would have faced had she not chosen to follow him. He should have known! He should never have trusted those men!

But even as she railed at him in her mind, a small voice chastised her:

Joining Stephen's crusade was your choice, it insisted. *Stephen did not even want you at first, have you forgotten? Only a handful of boys followed him then—he feared the journey would be too hard for a maid and that outraged you. You forced him to accept you. Do you not remember?*

It was true. She had to admit it.

"Angeline!" Father Martin called.

Startled out of her memories, she gave Stephen one last look, then made haste to catch up.

Alongside the riverbank the land was lush and green with trees and bushes and a small field in which grew some kind of crop.

Zeid pointed to the plants. "Al-fasfasah," he said. "The father of all foods."

Angeline stared at the low, bushy, green-leaved plants with pink flowers that she recognized immediately. Alfalfa, growing here, in this foreign land! The villagers grew it in France as well—the best of all fodder for their cattle, they believed. She reached down to touch a blossom. For one brief moment she could almost make herself believe that when she looked up again she would be back in her own village. That her mother would be calling her to sup. That this had all been naught but a nightmare. If only it could be true!

They walked on. As soon as they left the fertile banks, Zeid stopped.

"Behold," he said, gesturing.

Angeline caught her breath. Rolling, blinding dunes stretched out in front of her as far as the horizon. She was looking at a sea of sand as great as the sea over which they had sailed. Waves and waves of sand in every possible shade of light and dark. The sun blazed down so fiercely she had to shield her eyes; shimmers of heat wavered in the air. On the river there had been a slight breeze, but no air stirred here. Zeid had spoken truly. There was no escape. Beside her, Father Martin drew in his breath.

She stumbled as they made their way back to

the riverbank. It was just about the time the church bells in her village would have been sounding Vespers, and she saw not the dusty path on which she trod, but instead, the path she took every evening at this time to fetch water from the well in her village. People would be coming in from the fields, now. They would be settling down for their evening meals. Life would be continuing back in her village as it always had. How could that be? How could life go on as usual for them while she was so far away in such a different and terrifying world?

When they got back to the boat, Stephen still sat where they had left him. Father Martin approached and knelt beside him. He spoke, but Angeline could not hear what he said. Stephen took no notice, and with a sigh the priest straightened up again.

Then Angeline heard a lilting song coming from far up the river. It was strange and outlandish, like no other song she had ever heard before, in words she could not understand.

"You will wait now," Zeid said. He and the other men washed themselves in the river, then pulled out small rugs and prostrated themselves on them, foreheads to the ground.

This must be a call to prayer, Angeline thought. But prayer to a foreign god. She closed her eyes and ordered her mind to blot it out. In its place she tried to imagine the tolling of Christian bells, but to no avail. She could hear naught but the Muslim summons.

When their prayers were done, the men unpacked baskets of food and spread it out on cloths.

"Eat," Zeid said.

Father Martin settled himself down and motioned to Angeline to sit beside him. He glanced once at Stephen, then bowed his head and said grace. He prayed for a long time. When he had finished, Angeline looked at the food. Fruits and cheese. Loaves of round flat bread. Her stomach rose at the very sight of it.

"I cannot," she said.

No amount of entreating from Father Martin could change her mind. The priest made an attempt to eat, but she could see that he managed very little.

"You should try," Zeid said to her with a worried frown. "You need food."

Angeline shook her head.

After the meal was done, the boatmen erected two tents.

"One for the maiden," Zeid said. "You will sleep with the boatmen and myself," he added, motioning to Father Martin and Stephen.

Angeline crept into the shelter, grateful at first to have it to herself, but then lay fearful and loath to sleep. She was used to the close companionship they had developed on the crusade. She and Stephen had shared a campfire every night and rolled themselves in their cloaks side by side. Father Martin had always been right beside them, a reassuring presence. Usually at least two or three little ones had snuggled up to her for warmth and reassurance. On board the ship, even though it had been crowded and filthy, she had always been glad to have Stephen and Father Martin near. Now she felt so alone. She started at every small noise. Once she gathered the courage to peek out of the tent flap, but the darkness outside was impenetrable. Stars shone down out of a black sky with a brilliance she had never before seen. The invisible river gurgled past. Then a rustle in the trees above her head sent her scuttling back inside.

She had been given a roughly woven blanket and she wrapped herself in it. The day had been fiercely hot, but as soon as the sun set, all heat fled from the land and the night was cold. Sometime in the middle of the night the same lilting call to prayer echoed along the riverside again. Angeline heard Zeid and the boatmen come out of their tent to pray, but she huddled into her blanket and closed her eyes against them.

Finally, she slept.

Another call to prayer woke her the next

morning just at the time when her village bells would have been tolling Prime. She emerged from her tent to find Father Martin waiting, Stephen standing behind him.

"Come," the priest said, "it is time for us to pray, also."

"How can I pray?" Stephen said bitterly. "My God has deserted me." He turned from them and strode over to the boat.

Angeline stood helplessly, looking after him. Father Martin, too, stared after him, his face grim. Then he knelt. Angeline dropped to her knees beside him. She had come to trust and respect Father Martin, and the familiar words of the Mass should have comforted her, but she hardly heard them.

During that whole, terrible time, Stephen had never wavered in his belief. He had been steadfast in his purpose. Even when she had lost faith and chastised him, screamed at him in her despair over the deaths of the children, even then he had been as steady as a rock. But now he would not even pray! She bowed her head but her mind was spinning. She felt abandoned. Lost.

When they resumed their journey, Angeline made no further effort to talk to Stephen. She sat silently in the boat, staring at the shore as they swept by it. She could not bring herself to believe that what she was seeing was real. Everything was so different from anything she had known before. The banks along the river were a reddish colour. Here and there, nestled into the trees, were small huts made of mud bricks of the same hue. Women washed their clothing down by the water. She could hear their chattering as the boat sailed past. She saw donkeys and another one of the strange dun-coloured animals. Zeid pointed it out and told them that it was called a camel. "Gamal," in his own language. He seemed anxious to reassure them, to allay their fears, but when his arm brushed hers she flinched, still frightened of him. Oxen-like creatures pulled carts in the fields. Once she saw a boy herding sheep to the water. Stephen had been a shepherd. She glanced at him, then looked quickly away to spare him shame as she realized that he, too, was watching the boy and was weeping.

Then she saw a strange, fearsome beast slide into the water from the riverbank. Before her horrified eyes it began to swim toward them. Neither fish nor animal, it seemed to be a combination of both. It had a huge head and when it opened its mouth, Angeline saw long, sharp teeth, dripping water and green, slimy weeds. The creature was covered in what looked like scales. It swam nearer, its evil eyes fixed on her. She jumped to her feet and cried out. The boat rocked alarmingly.

Zeid caught her arm.

"Be still!" he commanded.

Father Martin reached for her other arm to steady her, but he was as frightened as she. His fingers dug into her skin painfully. Startled, Stephen half rose and stared at the thing. The boatmen, eyes wide with a terror as great as hers, made ready with their oars and pole to fend it off, but just as it reached the boat, it gave a flick of its powerful tail and disappeared under the water.

Angeline sank back down onto her seat, weak with shock. Unconsciously, she reached for Stephen's hand, but after his first start of alarm he had withdrawn again, his head buried in his arms.

The call to prayer sounded out twice more during the day before they camped for the second night. Each time the boatmen made the craft fast to the shore while they washed and prayed. Father Martin watched them, tight-lipped. The second time, around the middle of the day, Zeid and the boatmen ate a little bread and cheese. Father Martin accepted some, but Angeline still could not bring herself to eat. That night, however, her belly demanded food. She looked dubiously at the fruits spread out in front of her. They were strange to her. She picked up a bright, orange globe, not knowing what to expect. The rind was hard and slightly bitter, but when her teeth sank through, a burst of sweet juice filled her mouth. With that, her hunger suddenly overwhelmed her. She pulled the fruit apart greedily and sucked every drop from it. There were small, brown, sticky fruits as well. She tried them, avid now. When she bit into one of them her teeth grated on a hard pit, but again, the taste was so sweet that she spit out the stone and devoured the fruit. The cheese was white and crumbly. This was something she could recognize. It was not unlike the goat cheese she had eaten at home. She wrapped it in the flat bread and crammed it into her mouth. There was pale juice to drink that was tart on her tongue and refreshing. It quenched her thirst marvellously. When she finished, she licked her fingers clean and looked around. Father Martin was eating as well, but Stephen still sat in a stupor. She could not tell if he had eaten anything or not, but for the first time in months *her* belly was full. Starvation had killed many of the younger children on their crusade—there had never been enough food for all of them. She had usually given most of what little she could obtain to the smaller ones she had tried to care for.

Tried and failed. The thought thrust itself unbidden into her mind. How little Dominic would have enjoyed this feast. How the two angel-faced imps, Marc and Yves, would have gobbled it up.

The food she had eaten turned sour in her stomach. She staggered to her feet and vomited into the bushes beside their camp. The memory of those children—of all the lost children—was a searing ache within her that she would carry for the rest of her life.

Chapter Three

They reached Cairo on the third day. Angeline stared in horror at the confusion of people and animals on the dockside. It was even busier here than it had been in Alexandria; Cairo was obviously a great city. She allowed herself to be helped off the boat, then moved close to Father Martin and Stephen as the noise and the barrage of smells assaulted her.

"Follow me," Zeid commanded, and led the way into a narrow alley.

Angeline ducked her head to avoid the curious stares that followed them as they passed by. They had to hurry to keep up with Zeid as he led them through twisting, winding streets that teemed with people and animals. Donkeys clattered past, forcing them to give way. Carts rumbled, pulled by the oxen-like beasts she had seen working in the fields along the river. Heavily laden camels lumbered their way through the streets. Cats, too, slunk out of doorways and lazed on piles of merchandise. More cats than she had ever seen. Vendors shouted and called to Zeid as they passed, heavy scents of spices and foods that she had never smelled before filled her nostrils. Hundreds of people pushed and shoved their way around her, competing for space with each other and with the animals. Stephen walked as one in a dream, oblivious to everything around him. Father Martin held him by the arm and guided him, else he would surely have stumbled and fallen on the uneven cobblestones.

They passed a building richly decorated with coloured stone. Angeline thought it might be a church, it was so large, but it was much more ornate than the churches of her country and it was surmounted by four tall, onion-shaped spires. She had never seen anything like it. The beauty of its outline against the deep blue sky was such that she stopped and stared.

"That is a mosque," Zeid said. "Where we pray." He urged her forward.

Then she saw a man sumptuously attired in a vividly coloured gown ride by on a mule. Angeline could see jewels flashing on his fingers and she could not help but turn to watch him.

"A Christian," Zeid explained. "Probably one of the men who work for the administrators of the city. Many Christians do. They and the Jewish merchants are men of great wealth and importance. It is as I said—we live in peace together."

Angeline looked at Father Martin but he did not seem reassured.

"Coptic Christians," the priest muttered. "No better than heretics."

She had no idea what he meant.

They reached a street that seemed a bit more quiet than the others. There were no shops here; the street was lined with high, mud brick walls. By now Angeline's head was aching intolerably and her feet and ankles were covered in filth. Limp with the heat, she rubbed at her forehead. Stinging sweat ran down into her eyes. Flies were everywhere—a constant torment. Zeid led them to a doorway in one of the walls and rang a bell that hung outside. The door was opened by an elderly man—another slave, Angeline supposed—and they entered.

Inside all was in shadow. It was much cooler than the street outside. Angeline could hear the sound of falling water and as soon as the heavy door closed behind them all street noises disappeared. The street smells disappeared, too, to be replaced by a strange, pungent odour. She saw a stick burning in a dish and realized that must be where the scent was coming from. Angeline drew in a deep breath, trying to calm her racing heart, and wiped her sweaty hands on her shift. She braced herself for whatever was to happen next, but still she was unprepared when a veiled woman appeared and grasped her by the arm.

"Let me go!" she protested, and tried to pull away. To no avail. The woman's grip was too strong—her fingers dug into Angeline's flesh.

At that Stephen seemed to come to his senses.

"Angeline!" he cried.

Father Martin reached out for her, but Zeid barred his way.

"It is all right," Angeline heard him say. "She must go. She will come to no harm."

The words did not reassure Angeline. She struck out with her free hand, but the woman deflected her blow as easily as if she were naught but a small child, then dragged her to a curtained doorway set deep into the wall. Angeline made yet another attempt to get free, but there was no breaking the hold she was in. She cast one last despairing glance back at Stephen and Father Martin before she was hauled, stumbling, along a corridor and up a stone staircase. The floors upon which they walked were covered with deep carpets of intricate design. More such carpets hung on the walls around her. Never had Angeline seen such luxury, but it only filled her with more fear. What kind of people lived like this? They passed through a wooden screen and Angeline stared around her, speechless.

They were in a large room. Flowers were everywhere; the scent of fine perfumes mingled with their fragrance. A fountain sat in the middle of the tiled floor. Water cascaded down from it in a ceaseless flow. There were several women in the room and children played amongst them. Some of the women were lounging on cushions, two were playing what looked to be some sort of game with ivory pieces on a board. One woman plucked a kind of lute and music flowed out over all the chatter and laughter. The women were not veiled in here and the one who had accompanied Angeline unfastened her own veil as soon as the screen had shut behind them. Angeline could see now that she was older. Her face was full but creased with age. Her mouth, set in a thin line, did not look as if it had ever smiled. Angeline shrank away from her. As the woman pushed back the silken scarf that covered her head, Angeline saw that she had an abundance of thick, black hair, streaked with grey. It was pulled back from her face and fell almost to her waist, smooth and gleaming. Gold hoops swung from her ears.

The women in the room were mostly young. Some were dark-skinned, a few were as fair as Angeline herself. Some were even blonde. They were all dressed in brightly coloured, flowing gowns. Rings sparkled on their fingers, and to Angeline's astonishment, on their toes as well. They wore light sandals, mere straps. Obviously these were not shoes to be worn in the filthy streets. Were these concubines? Angeline wondered. Did the children belong to them?

They patted the children and played with them. Some women held babies and these were passed affectionately from one to another. There were four young girls, around the same age as herself, she thought. Not as sumptuously dressed as the older women—perhaps they were slaves, too? They ran toward her as soon as they saw her. The woman who had brought Angeline here said a few words, then motioned to Angeline to follow them. Instinctively, Angeline drew away from them, but the girls only laughed, then grabbed her and pulled her down a passageway and into another room that contained a large pool of water. Before she realized what they were about, they began to strip her shift off her. She pushed their hands away, but they just laughed even harder and continued disrobing her.

"Stop!" she cried, but to no avail.

She struggled but there were four of them and only one of her. Besides, they were plump and well-fed while she was thin and weak. In a trice they had stripped off her clothes and the ragged shoes she wore, and she stood before them, completely naked, crimson with shame.

One of the girls gathered up the clothes and shoes and disappeared, holding them by two fastidious fingers as far away from herself as possible, her nose wrinkled with disgust at the smell.

There was worse to come. The girls chattered and babbled to each other in a language that Angeline could not understand, but she understood when they motioned to her to get into the pool. She could not believe it. Submerge herself in that water? Completely? She shook her head vigorously. She had splashed water on her body now and then to clean herself off, but never voluntarily ventured all the way into any river or lake. No one in possession of all their senses would do so!

One of girls grabbed and tugged at her. Angeline ripped her arm out of her grasp. Another girl pushed her toward the water. Angeline pushed her back. Scowling, the girl shoved Angeline again, harder. Then the other girls seized her. Angeline kicked and screamed and even managed to bite one on the hand. That girl slapped her; she slapped back. Between the three of them they finally managed to drag Angeline into the water, but she dragged them in with her. It gave her great satisfaction to see them floundering in their light shifts that were now soaking wet and totally transparent. They were effectively as naked as she.

Her resistance did her no good, however. She found herself being scrubbed mercilessly with a soft, sweet-smelling soap. It was nothing like the harsh stuff made out of lye that was all she had ever seen before. They even lathered her hair. The bath had turned into a battle, but eventually it was over. She was finally allowed to climb out, dripping and swearing with every evil word she had ever heard. Then they attempted to dry her. Angeline seized the cloths from them, spitting with rage, and dried herself.

The one who had taken her clothes returned with a clean, brightly coloured shift and red leather slippers. She fairly threw them at Angeline. Angeline clothed herself as quickly as she could and bent to tie the slippers on her feet. She hardly noticed the softness of the material of the shift they had given her, nor the fineness of the slippers. The girls were not finished with her yet, however. Three of them held her while the fourth took a stiff brush and began to tear at the tangles in her hair. They were as rough as they could be, deliberately, she was certain of it. Tears sprang to her eyes in spite of herself, but she would not give them the satisfaction of seeing her cry. When she realized that the more she struggled, the more painful the task would be, she forced herself to hold still and endure it.

When they were done and had released her, she whirled around to face her tormentors. She glared at them. They glared back. Then she saw what they looked like. They were still soaking wet, their hair streamed water and their shifts clung to them in dripping folds.

They look like drowned rats, Angeline thought. Before she could stop herself, she began to laugh.

It was more hysteria than mirth, but even so, it enraged the girls. With one accord, they moved toward her, their eyes blazing with fury. The laughter died in Angeline's throat. They were about to tear her to pieces, she was sure of it.

At that moment the older woman returned. She looked at the angry girls, snapped out an order that caused them to fall back, then grasped Angeline's arm again and pulled her out of the room. Angeline was only too pleased to be out of there, but she would take no more of being pulled by the arm. She was beyond caring if the woman slapped her or not. She wrenched herself free. Then she forgot about that annoyance as another thought surfaced.

For what purpose had she been washed and prepared? For whom? She had heard stories around the campfires of the fearsome things that women captives of the heathen were subjected to. Now they flooded her mind in a sickening wave.

Chapter Four

The woman led Angeline down another corridor and then up a flight of stone steps. At the top she rapped on a door. A voice called from the other side. A female voice. Then the door opened.

To Angeline's amazement a small child stood in the opening. A girl, probably about five or six years old, but tiny. She had long, dark hair that fell in ringlets about her face and over her shoulders. Her face was tiny as well, with a sharply pointed little chin. She stared with huge dark eyes at Angeline, one finger in her mouth. Her other hand still clutched the door latch.

Angeline looked past her to see the person who had called out sitting at a table by a window. She had a book open in front of her and a pile of what looked like very fine parchment beside it. Angeline felt herself pushed forward.

The woman stood up. Angeline was surprised to see how tall she was. She was obviously the child's mother. The same dark, thick hair flowed loose upon her shoulders and she looked at Angeline with the same widely spaced, slightly tilted dark eyes. She said something in a questioning tone. Angeline had no idea what she wanted. Then the woman pointed to herself and said, "Ismi Zahra."

Zahra. Zeid had said that was the name of the woman for whom she had been bought. The concubine. The woman repeated her question. It seemed she was saying what her name was and asking Angeline's.

I won't answer, Angeline thought rebelliously.

Zahra raised one eyebrow and tilted her head to the side. She waited.

Angeline could not hold out against her.

"Angeline," she said, her voice as defiant as she could make it. "My name is Angeline."

Zahra smiled. She pointed to the woman waiting by the doorway and said, "Samah." Then she pointed to the small girl who still stared at Angeline. "Aza."

As Zahra pronounced the child's name, Aza pulled her finger from her mouth and ran to her. She clambered to be held and hid her face. Zahra pointed to the child and then to herself, gave the child a hug and said something else. Angeline supposed she must be saying that Aza was her daughter. Then Zahra laughed and held out her hand.

Angeline made no move to take it. Zahra dropped her hand, but did not seem annoyed. She motioned Angeline over to her. Angeline did not move. Instead, she clamped her mouth shut, aware that she looked sullen and stubborn. She wanted to. She wanted with every fibre of her being to defy this woman. To let her know that although she might think Angeline her slave, she was not.

No one can own me, Angeline told herself. I own myself. But again she was pushed from behind, this time not so gently. She stumbled forward.

Zahra cradled Aza with one arm and with the other, gestured toward the work on her table. Angeline could see now that she was copying from the book onto the parchment. Angeline had seen only one book before—the Holy Book that priests read from at Mass. She was astounded that a woman could possess one. And such a book! It was bound in soft leather, the pages were thin and fine. She could not read what Zahra was writing, of course, but as far as she could make out, Zahra was reproducing the strange, swirling characters on the pages of the book exactly. They looked more like beautifully drawn pictures than any writing she had ever seen. Zahra spoke to her, evidently explaining the work. Angeline kept her face blank. Zahra smiled again and gave a little shrug. Then she spoke a few words to Samah and motioned with her head for Angeline to go back to her.

Samah reached out to grasp her arm again; Angeline recoiled out of her reach. A torrent of words issued forth from Samah at that and she beckoned angrily for Angeline to follow her. It was either obey, or be hauled back down the passageway like a disobedient dog. Angeline obeyed, but she was seething with anger again.

They went back down another staircase, through a narrow passageway, and out into an open space in a covered courtyard where women were preparing food. A large mud brick oven stood in the centre and Angeline could smell bread baking over the fire beneath it. As they entered, a woman reached into the oven with a long wooden paddle and pulled out several round, flat loaves like the ones they had eaten on the journey to Cairo. Samah filled a tray with fruit and cheese, bowls of spicily scented meat, rice and beans, and rounds of the freshly baked bread. There were also small dishes of sweets and cakes. A jug of what looked to be some kind of juice sat in the middle of it all. Not the pale, yellow-coloured juice Angeline had drunk on the trip—this juice was a deep red in colour. Samah handed the tray to Angeline and spat out an order. It was not difficult to understand that she was to take it back to Zahra.

Angeline managed a quick nod and fled out of the cooking space, away from the pinching grasp of Samah's fingers. But then a new fear surfaced: could she find her way back to Zahra's room? The last thing she wanted was to have to return to Samah and ask, even if she could make herself understood. She looked around. Thankfully, at the end of the passageway she saw the staircase down which Samah had brought her.

At the top she hesitated again. Which way now? She plunged down the passageway leading to the right. A tapestry hanging on the wall there looked familiar. To her relief, she found herself in front of Zahra's door. She balanced the tray with one hand and knocked.

When she went in, Zahra said something which Angeline took to be a thank you, then indicated a low table where she could place the tray. Aza pounced on it immediately and snatched up one of the sweets. Zahra dragged a pillow over to the table and lowered herself gracefully onto it. She pulled Aza down beside her, said a few words which might have been a blessing, and began to eat.

Angeline stood awkwardly, watching and not certain of what she should do. When Zahra and Aza had finished, Zahra rose and went back to her work. She waved one hand at the leftover food and gave Angeline to understand that she could help herself to it.

Angeline flushed. Just so had her mother tossed crumbs to stray dogs. She set her mouth and shook her head. In any case, her stomach was in such a knot again that she could not have forced down even a bit of bread.

Samah returned and led Aza off. Zahra continued to work in silence. Angeline crouched in a corner and waited to see what would happen next.

At sunset she heard again the call to prayer. Zahra rose from her table and stretched. She moved over to another low bench on which sat a pitcher of water. She washed her hands and splashed water onto her face, then dried herself with a cloth that lay on the bench beside the pitcher. She unrolled a small, vibrantly coloured carpet. She placed this carefully on the floor, then prostrated herself to pray.

How strange, Angeline thought. These people

are heathens, but they obey their calls to prayer just as we Christians heed the pealing of our church bells. She looked out the window to the crimson and gold sky beyond. A flight of pigeons flew past, their wings breaking the call of the prayer into echoes. The anger that she had been nurturing so determinedly was suddenly gone. In its place—a longing so sharp that she drew in her breath with a gasp of pain. This was the reality of it. Never again would she hear those church bells.

"Help me, oh Lord." She whispered. "Help me."

Zahra began to make her preparations for the night. Angeline watched uncertainly, not knowing what she should do. Then Zahra indicated a pallet in the corner of the room. Angeline sidled over to it and sat hesitantly down on the edge. She would sleep here then, it seemed. At that, a new and embarrassing worry surfaced. Zahra seemed to be settling down to sleep, but Angeline had to relieve herself. Where should she go? How could she make her need known?

As if divining her thoughts, Zahra pointed to a screen in the opposite corner of the room. To

Angeline's relief it concealed an ornately decorated pot. She used it, then made her way back to her cot. Zahra lay in her bed; a wick burning low beside her gave the only light to the room. Angeline's pallet lay in deep, flickering shadows. She lowered herself onto it, then lay down and curled up tightly, hands hugging her knees close to her chest.

Zahra said a few words—perhaps bidding her a good night—but Angeline knew not how to answer so she kept silent. In a short time the woman's soft, steady breathing indicated that she slept. Angeline, however, remained tense and stiff. Her mind spun wildly.

Where were Stephen and Father Martin? What was happening with them? Were they being well treated? The questions tumbled around in her brain, over and over, but the softness of the cushions upon which she lay was seductive and she was exhausted. In spite of herself, she felt sleep creeping over her. The pallet was small but more comfortable than anything she had known. A long strand of her hair fell over one arm. Washed cleaner than ever before, it glinted golden in the flickering flame. She looked at it in wonder. She had had no idea her hair was so fair. Her last thought before sleep overcame her was that for the first time in her life she did not itch. She was not scratching and picking the vermin off her legs and arms.

She did not hear the call to prayer during the night. Zahra must have prayed then, but she did not call Angeline to attend her. She did wake Angeline with the morning prayer, however. She washed, then waved Angeline out the door—Angeline could only suppose she was to go again for food. She made her way back to the cooking area where the women had Zahra's tray ready for her, then took it back upstairs. Once more, when Zahra had finished, she indicated that Angeline might partake of what was left over. The amount of food provided was ample and by now Angeline's hunger proved stronger than her pride. She helped herself liberally to the rice and beans and fruit. She sipped hesitantly at the juice. Never had she seen juice so deep a crimson colour. She could not imagine what fruit it came from, but it was sweet and refreshing. She drank a brimming cupful and then, seeing that Zahra was not watching her, she made bold to pour herself another and drank that as well.

After they had finished and Angeline had returned the tray to the cooking area, Zahra began to make ready for the day. She put on a gown made of the flimsiest, lightest silk. It was embroidered all over with gold flowers and silver stars. She handed Angeline a brush. Her hair was still mussed from sleep and Angeline bridled. Did the woman really expect her to brush it for her? It seemed she did. She smiled and gestured to Angeline to begin, but when Angeline made no attempt to comply, the smile disappeared. She snapped out a command and frowned. Rebelliously, Angeline began. She almost gave in to the impulse to snag the knots roughly, then she stopped herself. This woman had power over her. Whether Angeline liked it or not, she would have to obey. She did not know what the consequences would be otherwise, but she had a feeling that they would not be pleasant.

Zahra unstoppered a small flask and dabbed a heady, fragrant oil on her wrists, between her breasts, and behind her earlobes. Angeline did not rebel any further. She helped, handed Zahra what she asked for, and watched, amazed. Never had she seen such elaborate preparations. Never had she seen such indulgence! She thought back to her own mother. Marithe was always up with the dawn, but she needed no one to help her prepare for the day. She wore the shift she slept in and a splash of water on her face was the extent of her morning ablutions. She was nearly always hard at work by the time Angeline had rubbed the sleep from her eyes. How soft this woman was!

When Zahra was ready, she motioned to Angeline to follow her. She left the room and retraced the way to the harem. There, the other concubines greeted her warmly and with great courtesy. Angeline was quick-eyed, however, and did not miss seeing two of the women exchange a sidelong glance. From the twist of their downturned mouths, Angeline surmised that Zahra was not as universally loved as they might pretend. But if Zahra noticed, she did not show it. She smiled back at them all, and allowed them to plump up cushions for her and bring her a dish of sweets dripping with honey.

The four slave girls were there and they gave Angeline sour looks when they saw her. They, at least, made no pretense of friendship. Angeline glared back at them.

At one end of the room, a tangle of children played, supervised by Samah. One of them looked up; it was Aza. Aza saw Zahra at the same time and tore herself free from her playmates. She threw herself upon her mother. Zahra hugged her and smothered her with kisses, laughing all the while.

For the rest of the morning, Zahra amused herself with the other women. Angeline stood by and did whatever Zahra asked her to do. She fumed with resentment but she hid it. More important now was to find out what had happened to Stephen.

Zahra was the only concubine who seemed to have her own slave. The four girls tended to the other women, running errands for them, fetching scarves or other necessities as was required. At one point Angeline found herself in the cooking area with one of the girls—Anka, she had heard her called. Zahra had made Angeline understand that she wished her to fetch more juice. Anka sneered at Angeline and said something to the cooking women that made them laugh. Angeline flushed. She took up the pitcher they gave her and turned to go back. At that moment Anka stuck out her foot and tripped her. Angeline went sprawling. The pitcher fell and broke, the juice spilled. Anka had done it so craftily, however, that none of the women had seen what happened. They advanced on Angeline, shouting and furious. One of them even struck her. It was only by abasing herself completely and making begging signs that Angeline managed to get them to give her another pitcher of juice. The resentment brewing within her threatened to boil over. She would gladly have torn Anka's hair out by the roots, but Anka had been canny enough to take herself off.

Before the call to prayer at noon, the time when her own church would have been announcing Sext, Zahra led Angeline back to her room, taking Aza with her. After their midday meal, Zahra lay down on her couch to sleep away the hottest hours of the day, Aza beside her. She indicated that Angeline could rest, too, but there was no sleep for Angeline. Instead, she lay on the cushions which now seemed sweltering and smothering. Was this how her life was to end? A slave. A life of servitude. To Zahra, or perhaps to some other. She would have no control over what happened to her. Perhaps Zeid had spoken truly when he said that she was fortunate to be Zahra's slave, but what if she displeased Zahra in some way? She could not understand her—it was not likely that she ever would. She could make no sense of this language at all!

What if she were sold to someone far less kind? Many of the other concubines in the harem were quick to slap or find fault with the other slave girls there; Angeline could not suppose they would treat a slave of their own any better. She was caged in with these women as surely as if she had been bound and thrown into a prison.

Underlying all these worries was one thought that kept pushing itself into her mind, no matter how hard she tried to stave it off. What if she were never to see Stephen again? She would not be able to bear that. He had been her constant companion for months. She had come to depend on him for everything, but he had been so despairing—had Father Martin been able to comfort him?

He was all she had left—she could not lose him!

Chapter Five

Zahra woke with the mid-afternoon call to prayer and made ready to work. To distract Aza and keep her amused, she handed the child a quill and some scraps of spoiled parchment. Aza immediately began to fill the pages with scribbles, dribbling as much ink over herself as onto the parchment. Zahra laughed and held the ink bottle out to Angeline. Angeline hastened to take it and help guide Aza's hand more accurately.

To Angeline's amazement, she discovered that the pages were not parchment made from the skins of animals, but something much finer. Seeing her curiosity, Zarah gave her a quill as well. Angeline took it hesitantly, unsure as to whether Zahra really meant for her to draw, too. She had sometimes drawn pictures for her mother on old discarded skins with charcoal from the fire, however, and she knew she had a talent for it. It had given her and her mother both much merriment. At Zahra's nod of encouragement, she drew a cat for Aza. It was much easier to work on this fine paper than on the rough skins. The child looked at the cat and crowed with delight. She pushed the paper back to Angeline, saying a word over and over. Angeline could not understand her, but it was obvious what she meant.

"More. More."

Angeline drew the white birds that she had seen swooping along the riverbanks. Then she drew a donkey and some sheep. She drew a camel, but could not properly remember what those beasts looked like and Aza laughed at it. Then she drew the awesome beast that had slithered into the water after their boat. She drew only its eyes above the water and a swirl where the tail was. She made it as fierce as she could and Aza screamed in mock terror. Without realizing it, Angeline began to enjoy the play.

When Aza tired of this, Angeline sat her down and made her understand with hand gestures that she wanted her to sit still. This Aza managed to do, but only for a moment. Angeline swiftly sketched the child's face. She had never before attempted to capture anyone's features and she watched her work develop with astonishment as, with what seemed almost like a will of their own, her fingers flew over the paper. There were Aza's eyes looking out at her, Aza's mouth smiling at her.

Aza could not wait to see what Angeline had drawn. Before the drawing was finished, she tore the page from Angeline's hands and pranced over to Zahra with it. Zahra gave the drawing a glance, then looked at it more sharply. She looked back up at Angeline. She gave a quick nod and said something that sounded like praise. In spite of herself, Angeline felt a small surge of pride.

For just a few moments Angeline had forgotten where she was, even forgotten Stephen and Father Martin, but when Aza settled down to playing with a few beads and trinkets in a box that Zahra gave her, everything flooded back.

She watched Zahra working. The woman wrote with a fierce concentration, brow furrowed and the tip of her tongue caught between her teeth. How could Angeline make her understand that she had to find out what had happened to Stephen? She had to see him!

"My God has betrayed me," he had said. How could he possibly utter such words? He who had had such faith. Such blinding belief. She remembered the nights they had sat together by their fire after he had preached to his followers. On those nights they had talked long into the darkness, and on one of them he had told her about his vision—although he did not believe it to be a vision.

"It was not a man who came to me in that field," he had said. "It was the Christ Himself."

"How did you know?" Angeline had asked him, hardly daring to whisper the question.

"I knew," Stephen had answered. "I looked into His face and I knew."

He had not wavered in his purpose, not even when King Philip had refused to help him. She closed her eyes and could see him right now, hear his words as clearly as if he spoke them in this room at this very moment.

"I made a vow to God," Stephen had said. "I left my sheep. I left my father. I left my brother. I left everything I had ever known to follow God's will."

But had it really been God's will that hundreds—thousands—of children and young people should die along the way?

"They are with God," Father Martin and the other priests had said. "It is not for us to question the will of God."

But Angeline did question. She wrapped her

arms around herself and shivered with the remembrance of the days and nights of cold and hunger. The avarice and predation of most of the adults who had joined them. Joined them not to liberate Jerusalem, but to prey on the children. To use them and abuse them, to sell them, even, to the villagers in the towns they passed through. She herself had narrowly escaped injury. She shuddered at that memory.

It had happened one day when she had nearly swooned with hunger. She had stumbled over to a rock and sunk down upon it. Stephen had been ahead of her; he had not noticed that she had fallen back. She had stared after him, about to call out, but she was too weak even to do that. She would rest a while, she had thought, then catch them up. They disappeared around a bend in the road. It had made her anxious to see them go, but she could not summon the strength to follow. She closed her eyes. Then she heard laughter.

A group of men and women had been coming down the road toward her. The woman were loud and slovenly. They were laughing at jokes the men were making. Angeline heard and cringed at the coarseness of their talk. She had closed her eyes again and gathered into herself, waiting for them to pass, but they did not pass. The voices, the laughter, surrounded her and did not go away.

She winced now at the memory of the rough hand on her shoulder. Before she could shake it off she had been pushed to the ground and a heavy, panting man threw himself down upon her.

"Now we shall have some sport!" he had cried.

She felt stones crushing into her spine. She beat at him with her fists, but he only laughed all the more. Desperately, she had looked to the faces surrounding her. The women, surely they would help her! She had cried out, but they laughed even louder than the men. Their faces swam in her vision, they melted into each other. She heard a roaring in her ears, a black mist rose behind her eyes. She felt the man's hands upon her, tearing at her shift.

And then a voice. A voice thundering with rage. The man who had her pinned to the ground cried out as a stick struck his back.

"Be off with you! Swine! Worse than swine! Be off with you, I say!"

Father Martin, a towering figure of rage, was striking out at first one and then another of the men.

Black crow indeed, she had thought, irrationally, as the darkness closed in upon her.

When she had come to her senses, Father Martin was bathing her forehead with water. A circle of frightened children's faces stared down at her. Stephen knelt beside her, his face stricken and white. He looked older than Father Martin.

"I thought you to be dead!" he had cried.

That night Stephen himself had made up a thin soup for her. It was no more than water with a few roots and herbs thrown in, but it had revived her somewhat. He had stayed with her until all the others were asleep.

"Are you certain you are all right?" he had asked, over and over. "You are not hurt?"

"I am well," Angeline had answered.

But she had not been well. She was sick to her soul. Dominic was dead. Yves and Marc were dead. All who had started out with them were gone. And more. So many, many more.

Stephen had seemed to know what she was thinking. She remembered now how he had dropped his head into his hands. How his shoulders shook.

"It was not supposed to be like this," he had whispered. "It was not supposed to be like this."

She did not wonder that Stephen despaired. Only, she wanted to go to him now. To help him.

She opened her eyes and looked again at Zahra. Somehow she must make her understand. Slowly, she got to her feet and walked over to the woman. She stood beside her, unsure of what to do next. Zahra, suddenly aware of her, looked up. She frowned, obviously annoyed at being interrupted.

"Stephen," Angeline said. "My friend . . ."

Zahra stopped her with a short, quick word. She pointed back to Aza and, with a wave of her hand, indicated that Angeline should go back to the child.

"But I must see him . . ." Angeline persisted, knowing even as she spoke that it was useless.

Zahra snapped out another word, now clearly angry at the interruption. Angeline clamped her mouth shut and returned to Aza. She would be silent for now; she had no choice. But she would try again. And again. Until somehow she could make her need to see Stephen known. She had to.

The child clambered onto Angeline's knee, put her finger in her mouth, and nestled her head into Angeline's neck. She cuddled Aza close to her and buried her face in the child's hair. Just so had she held poor, small Dominic on the night before he died. The youngest of all the children he had been, and one of the first to join the crusade.

Samah returned to fetch Aza before the evening prayer. Then it was time for Angeline to go for

Zahra's meal. She set the tray on the low table and looked at Zahra warily, but Zahra seemed to have recovered from her annoyance. She looked up and said a word that by now seemed familiar to Angeline.

"Shukran."

Perhaps it meant "thank you."

Zahra beckoned Angeline over to her work table. Angeline would have dearly loved to disobey, but she knew she could not. Stifling her bitterness, she moved to stand beside Zahra. What order would she give now? But, to Angeline's surprise, Zahra did not want anything. Instead, she wrote some symbols down on another scrap of paper, then handed the quill to Angeline and indicated that she should copy them.

Suspicious, but curious as well, Angeline set the quill to the paper and copied the symbols as best she could. Zahra seemed pleased. She pointed to the characters Angeline had copied and repeated the word. "Shukran." Angeline realized that must be what she had written. She stared at it. She had written a word!

After the meal, Zahra returned to her work. She gave Angeline no further orders. At a loss for something to do, Angeline picked up her quill again and began to draw the faces of the four slave girls. She warmed to her task—it was one way of letting out the frustration and anger that filled her to such an extent that she felt she must explode with it. She gave the girls such sour expressions that they looked like the ugliest of old crones. Serves them right, she thought. She made Anka especially ugly.

But all the time she kept sneaking looks at the word she had written. She had written a *word.* She could read it. She wanted to do more.

The next day, after Zahra had broken her fast, Angeline resolved to find out where Stephen was and how he fared. She *had* to or she would go mad. She could not just go about her day-to-day duties without knowing where he was or how he was being treated. Somehow, she would have to make Zahra understand. She was just about to speak when Samah appeared in the doorway. Before Angeline could say anything, Zahra motioned to her to follow the servant woman. Angeline hesitated, but Samah snatched at her arm, and with a vicious pinch, hurried her out the door. There was nothing for it but to follow.

Samah led Angeline down the passageway to a different part of the house. They went through an opening covered with a hanging tapestry and Angeline found herself walking along a balcony that ran around the upper floor. It surrounded an inner courtyard that was open to the sky. Angeline was instantly alert. This was the first time she had been in any part of the house other than the women's quarters.

The courtyard was filled with flowers and lush bushes. A vine starred with white flowers climbed up to the balcony and encircled around it. The blossoms gave off a heady, heavy sweet perfume. A fountain stood in the centre; water cascaded down from it into a pool. Cobbled walks spread out from the fountain to each corner where fringe-leaved trees gave shade to benches set beneath them. Small, brilliantly coloured birds flashed in and out of the trees like living jewels. A cat lay draped on one of the benches, watching them idly and soaking up the sun. An old man dug in a flower bed; a boy worked beside him. Angeline glanced at them, then drew in her breath with a gasp. Surely that boy . . . Yes! It . . . was!

"Stephen!" she cried.

Stephen looked up, startled. Samah hissed in anger. She grabbed Angeline and wrenched her away from the balcony railing. At the same time she gave Angeline a slap that sent her head reeling. Before Angeline could recover her senses, she had been pulled through another doorway that led off the balcony and down yet another staircase. At the bottom of this, Angeline saw the door through which they had been brought into the house. A slave sprang to open it. Samah pulled her through and Angeline found herself back in the street. She had time for no more than one anguished backward glance before Samah tugged her on.

But she had seen him. That old man must have been the gardener Zeid had said Stephen was to work with. She had seen Stephen! And she would again, she vowed. In her mind she retraced the path they had taken from the women's quarters to that balcony. One way or another, she would find the means to get back there.

When the door shut behind them they were immediately plunged back into the noisy chaos of the city. Angeline ducked as a cart rumbled past. She had no idea where they were going. She picked her way carefully through the filth as Samah led her along narrow streets paved with stones. However resentful she was at being forced into slavery, she had grown fond of her bright red slippers and did not want to soil them.

There was no thought of escape here. Where would she go? She was already so confused that she would not even have been able to find her way back to the Emir's house. Dwellings crowded on either side of the street, many with balconies that overhung the roadway. She dodged donkeys pulling carts and bell-laden camels carrying water up from the river. Samah forged ahead, oblivious to the people she elbowed out of her way. She made a turn and they were in a market. The streets were wider here, lined on both sides with stalls. Vendors shouted out their wares; customers shouted back. At the far end Angeline could see the minarets of another mosque rising up to the sky.

Angeline was overwhelmed at first and confused, then she began to realize that there was order around her in spite of the noise. Each street was assigned a different trade. They passed through alleys full of fresh fruits and vegetables, then through a passageway lined with leather-makers' stalls. There were booths offering spices, bolts of cloth, even jewels that blazed and sparkled in the sunlight. A carpet maker had spread some of his fine samples out on the street and urged people to walk on them. Other carpets hung on both sides of his stall and covered the walls within, making a cave of luxurious, riotous colour.

Finally, at the end of the market, just in front of the mosque, they came upon the perfume makers. Here Samah stopped. She made her way purposefully to one particular stall. On display were dozens of delicate glass bottles of every size, shape, and colour, from tiny flasks no taller than Angeline's little finger to flagons big enough to hold a cupful of liquid. Myriad scents set Angeline's head swimming. Samah, however, seemed to know exactly what she wanted. Without hesitation she reached for a small flask filled with a golden liquid. She unstoppered it, raised it to her nose, and sniffed, then nodded with satisfaction. She held it out to Angeline. Angeline took a deep whiff. It was the same heady fragrance that Zahra wore. Samah spoke to the vendor. He answered her. She spoke again, more sharply. He raised his hands to the sky as if imploring mercy and let loose a torrent of words. Samah was a match for him, however, and gave him back just as good a flood. Angeline realized what was going on. Just so had she been bargained for and sold.

Finally, Samah reached into a pouch that hung at her waist and pulled out some coins. The vendor weighed them on his scale and, feigning anguish, accepted them. Immediately the two were fast friends. The vendor showed Samah to a stool and shooed a cat off it. He clapped his hands. A young boy appeared bearing a tray with the crimson juice that by now Angeline had learned was made with the blossoms of a flower, not fruit. He offered it to Samah. She sipped it and babbled a stream of words back to the vendor. Angeline picked out "shukran" amongst them. It was only one word, but at least there was something here she could understand.

When the flask had been wrapped in a brightly coloured cloth and handed to Angeline to carry, they turned and made their way home.

Angeline made ready to call out to Stephen as soon as they entered the house. She cared not what Samah would do to her and she was prepared to fight if the woman tried to drag her away again. But Samah led her back to Zahra's room by a different way. She had no chance.

Chapter Six

One night Zahra did not make ready for bed after the evening prayer. Instead, she beckoned to Angeline to assist her in changing into a soft, clinging gown. Angeline had escorted her to the bath, the "hamman" it was called, earlier in the day. Angeline had grown used to this strange custom of bathing the whole body. The slaves and servants had their own hamman—the smaller bath where she had been scrubbed when she arrived. They were allowed to use it after their duties for the day were done and Angeline had to admit that she actually looked forward to it now. She enjoyed the sensation of being clean, and she certainly enjoyed the absence of fleas.

Zahra had Angeline brush her hair until it stood out in soft waves all around her face. Then she took up a small pot made from translucent, pink stone. It was filled with fine, black powder. Angeline watched, fascinated, as Zahra picked up a short silver stick and moistened it with water in which rose petals soaked. Then she dipped the stick into the powder, and to Angeline's further astonishment, put the stick in the corner of her eye. She closed her eye over it and drew it straight across. Angeline winced, but it did not seem to hurt Zahra at all. She leaned forward to check her reflection in a silver mirror and was satisfied only when both eyes were nicely black around the roots of her eyelashes. When she looked up her eyes were dark and mysterious. She laughed at the expression that Angeline knew must be on her face.

"Kuhl," she said, indicating the black powder. Then she went to the door and signalled for Angeline to follow her.

Puzzled, but on the alert as ever for a sight of Stephen, Angeline followed Zahra to a part of the house she had not yet seen. They came to a curtain that blocked the hallway. Zahra pushed it aside and held it back so that Angeline could follow her in. Angeline caught her breath. Oil lamps burned in intricately decorated alcoves set into the walls. Bowls of silver and gold reflected their flickering light. Angeline's feet sank into a thick, brilliantly woven carpet. Where the floor was bare, she trod on tiles glazed in shades of blue, indigo, and green. Tapestries covered the walls. In one corner sat a chest shining with inlaid jewels. A glass lamp hung above it. In another corner of the room a brass dish hung suspended, a slender stick burning within it. The stick gave off a scent with which Angeline was becoming familiar. It was a scent at once sharp and sweet. Sticks such as this burned in most rooms. They perfumed the air and seemed to keep flying insects at bay. Angeline looked around her in awe, then stifled a startled cry as she saw a man clad in a long, flowing robe sprawled on a pile of pillows.

A servant stood beside the man, holding a tray upon which a cup of juice waited. The man smiled and rose to his feet. Zahra went to him and he bent to embrace her. Angeline felt the blood rush to her head and her face flush. This must be Abd'al Haseeb, the Emir himself! He was much younger than Angeline had expected. She had imagined him to be aged, but this man was not much older than Father Martin. Not a gentle-looking man, though, as was Father Martin. His eyes as he looked at Zahra softened, but there was nothing else soft about his face or his expression. His cheekbones were sharp, his skin dark. He had the look of a man who lived much outdoors under the desert sun. The arm with which he encircled Zahra was sinewy and strong. No idle prince—Angeline could believe that this Emir was a fighting man.

They took no notice of her, but disappeared through a curtained doorway. Angeline was left standing in the room unsure of what to do. The servant came over to her and motioned to a carpet lying in front of the doorway, piled with pillows. She realized that he meant for her to settle there. Shock was replaced by anger. She was supposed to sleep outside their room like a dog?

"I will not!" she cried, heedless of the fact that the servant would not understand her words. He would certainly know what she meant. But he just smiled and left.

She ran to the doorway that led back out into the hall, but another servant there firmly escorted her back to her pillows. Furious, but helpless to resist, she threw herself down upon them. She sat there, determined not to sleep, but finally, when the midnight prayer sounded through the rooms, she succumbed in spite of herself.

She was awoken by a servant bearing a tray of food. He greeted her and held the tray out to her.

Was she supposed to carry it in to Zahra and the Emir? Another wave of hot shame suffused her. How could she do such a thing? Without waiting for her consent, the servant swept back the curtain and opened the door beyond it, then gently pushed Angeline in. She took a hesitant step, not daring to raise her eyes. Zahra's voice greeted her. Only then did she look up. Zahra was sitting at a low table, the Emir lay on a couch beside her. They were both wearing long, hooded robes. He was watching Zahra and took no notice of Angeline at all. Zahra indicated the table. Angeline placed the tray of food upon it. She could not look again at the Emir. Zahra chose carefully from amongst the dishes and carried a selection over to Abd'al Haseeb, then she waved Angeline back out of the room. Angeline escaped with relief. She waited outside the door, unwilling to sit again, not knowing what she should do and furious at the indignity.

When Zahra finally came out they returned to her room. Angeline helped her dress and make ready for the day. Zahra kept up a constant chatter, but Angeline attended her in stony silence. She made no effort to understand the concubine. She did not want to understand her. How could Zahra have humiliated her so?

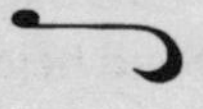

When they settled for their afternoon nap, Angeline was still seething. She hated being a slave. She hated the indignity of waiting on such people. She hated Zahra. She lay on her couch, fuming, listening to Zahra's deep, even breaths. Aza lay close to her mother, snuffling slightly in her sleep.

And then it occurred to her. Zahra would sleep now for at least an hour. Why not slip out? She had no thought of escape, but she could find her way back to that courtyard. She could at least see Stephen. She half rose, watching Zahra and Aza, ready to quickly lie back down if either one of them showed any sign of awakening. She got to her feet and stood motionless for a moment. She could still use the excuse that she had to use the pot behind the screen to relieve herself if Zahra opened her eyes and saw her.

She took a few cautious steps toward the door, then, growing more bold, she reached for the latch and opened it as quietly as she could. In the next moment she had slid out and carefully pulled the door shut behind her.

The house was silent, drowsy with heat. She could not hear a sound anywhere. Perfect. She took a second to rehearse the way in her mind, then set out. It took only moments for her to reach the balcony. She rushed to the railing and looked over, then suppressed an exclamation of disappointment. The courtyard was empty.

Of course. How could she have been so witless? No doubt Stephen and the gardener were also granted a rest during this hottest time of day. She stood for a moment longer, unwilling to give up. If only Stephen would come. If only he would somehow or other decide to work anyway. And then, as she watched, she saw a movement in the corner of the garden. Was it Stephen? Hope stirred within her and she leaned far forward, only to meet the eyes of the slave girl, Anka, who was gathering flowers, probably for one of the concubines.

They stared at each other, startled, then Anka ran back into an opening that led off the courtyard. For a moment Angeline stood frozen, too surprised to move, then a pang of fear knifed through her. Had Anka gone to inform on her? She had to get back to Zahra! She turned and ran.

In her haste she went down the wrong corridor. For a moment she panicked, then retraced her steps and found her way again, but she had lost precious time. When she reached Zahra's room, the door stood ajar. She could hear Samah's voice, loud and accusing. Anka must have run straight to her. Angeline almost fled, but that would only make matters worse. She tightened her hands into fists to hide their shaking, held her head as high as she could, and entered.

Samah exploded with anger when she saw her. Zahra's eyes blazed. Aza crouched on the bed behind her mother, eyes wide with anxiety. Zahra dismissed Samah with one curt word. Samah brushed past Angeline, glaring at her and muttering. Angeline braced herself. Zahra looked furious. She strode past Angeline, shut the door, locked it, then dropped the key onto the table where she kept her perfumes and cosmetics. She pointed to Angeline's couch and snapped out an order. It was obvious what she meant. Angeline walked over to the couch with as much dignity as she could muster but, as she sank down onto it a hard, cold ball seemed to grow and expand in her chest until she could hardly breathe. She would be given no further chance to leave this room unsupervised, that was certain. What other punishments might be in store for her?

Aza bounced off the bed and began to run toward her. Zahra caught her and pulled her back down onto the pillows. She spoke sharply to her—more sharply than Angeline had ever heard her address her daughter. Chastened, Aza curled back up, finger in her mouth. Zahra lay down beside her and, without another word, drew the child close to her and closed her eyes to resume her sleep. Angeline felt as if she had been slapped. She sat, staring at them. From beneath Zahra's arms, Aza stared back.

When Samah returned later to fetch Aza she was still glowering. Angeline glowered back. Slave she might be to Zahra, but she was neither slave nor servant to Samah.

The next morning Zahra seemed to have recovered most of her good humour. She sent Angeline to the cooking place as usual, but with words that sounded much like a warning. Angeline took heed. She returned with Zahra's breakfast, then stood silently by while Zahra ate. She was relieved that there did not seem to be any further consequences coming for her disobedience. At the same time, she still burned with resentment. Why should she be at the mercy of these people?

As soon as she entered the harem she saw Anka and the other three slave girls, Nabeela, Raful, and Heba. They were huddled together in the farthest corner. When they caught sight of her, Anka whispered a few words and they hid their mouths behind their hands and giggled. Anka looked straight at her and smiled a smug, triumphant grin.

One of the other concubines called to the girl. Too occupied with sneering at Angeline, Anka did not hear her. The woman strode over to her and slapped her. Anka gave a small cry of pain. Now it was Angeline's turn to gloat, and gloat she did.

But that night Angeline lay on her couch listening to the soft night sounds outside their window long after Zahra slept. The wick in the dish of oil beside her bed was almost consumed. It sputtered and died, then flamed again to cast strange dancing shadows on the walls around her.

She had never thought that her mother would die. Their life had been poor and some would have said hard, but it had not seemed so to Angeline. They had their garden for vegetables. Marithe was an accomplished seamstress, and the townsfolk supplied them with meat and other necessities in return for the garments she sewed for them. As far as Angeline knew, her life was full and satisfying. She ran free through the woods and fields around their village. She had believed Marithe would always be there to protect her, to soothe her ills and rub her bumps and injuries away with the calming salves that she made.

Angeline had hated sewing and avoided it as much as possible. Marithe understood, and while Angeline was growing to maidenhood, she had let her daughter go her own way. She had delighted in the untidy bunches of wildflowers the child brought home to her, and she welcomed the roots and berries that Angeline discovered to eke out their meagre suppers. They had had a good life. But of course the villagers disapproved of Angeline's wild ways.

"Just like her mother," they said, but never to her face.

Her mother had known well what the talk was but Marithe just laughed and let the girl enjoy herself. People were glad to wear the garments Marithe sewed for them; that was enough for her. Only, Angeline had never known who her father was. She asked once, but her mother would not answer her.

"He left," was all she had said. "He moved on and left me with the most precious gift God could have given me. You."

Angeline could have asked around the town, but she would not give pleasure to the many sharp-tongued women who would have taken great delight in telling her all the details of her mother's folly, for folly it surely was. Otherwise, Marithe would have been properly wed as were the rest of them.

As she lay in the shifting darkness, Angeline tried to recall her mother's face. To her dismay, she realized that she could no longer see her clearly. She pulled a sheet of paper over to her and a quill. By the flickering light of the dying wick she began to sketch but, try as she might, the face she drew never seemed right.

It was too late—she had forgotten too much.

She crumpled up the paper and threw it on the floor. Zahra would be provoked at the waste, but she did not care. As the wick finally guttered out, she gave herself up to her sorrow and collapsed back onto the pillows. She wept then as she had not allowed herself to weep in all the time since Marithe had died.

She was saying farewell. Farewell to her mother, farewell to all of her old life. And farewell to Stephen's magnificent dream of rescuing Jerusalem.

Did he weep, too, in these long hours?

Chapter Seven

Over the next few days Angeline realized that Zahra was keeping a close watch on her. She allowed Angeline out of her sight only to go to the cooking place to fetch her food. Angeline chafed at this and, even though she knew full well she was being unreasonable, she took offense at Zahra's distrust. She was wild with impatience to see Stephen, to speak with him. Several times she had tried to make Zahra understand what she wanted, but Zahra either would not or could not do so. Then one morning Zahra sent her again to the market—the "suq,"

Angeline had learned it was called—with Samah. Angeline did not allow herself to hope that Samah would let her anywhere near that balcony again, nor did she.

When they reached the suq, Samah led Angeline to the alley where spices were sold. Here were stalls with shelves upon shelves of baskets containing all manner of spices, none of which Angeline had ever seen before coming to Egypt. She was beginning to recognize some of them by now, however. The long reddish-yellow threads were saffron. The cooking women used them in rice, turning it to the same golden hue. She knew not the names of the others, but could recognize some of them by their scents. Spicy cloves, ground powders, seeds in every colour. The mingled smells were wonderful, yet almost overpowering. Samah made her selection carefully. She chose, also, a whole basket of the dried flowers that were used to make the sweet, crimson juice that Angeline had already become fond of.

After being shut up for so long, Angeline allowed herself to relax and soak up the sunlight and the bustle. She even found herself enjoying the crowds of shouting, boisterous people. It was so alive! While Samah bargained with the spice seller, Angeline began to tempt a small cat toward her by dangling a string in front of its nose. The kitten watched her warily for a time, then could resist no longer and lunged forward. It batted the string with a lightning stroke of one paw, then whisked itself back behind a basket where it peeked out, eyes bright, ears alert. Angeline giggled. Then she caught herself. She had laughed! She could not remember the last time she had laughed out of sheer merriment!

Samah finally came to terms with the spice seller, then began to load Angeline up with the basket and various packets of spices. At that moment, Angeline heard an even greater shouting than usual, accompanied by the clamour of bells. She looked up to see a crowd of jeering, guffawing people pushing down the street toward them. Two men were leading a donkey with another man riding backwards on it. This unfortunate man wore a tall, red hat, festooned with bells. As Samah pulled Angeline aside to let them pass, Angeline saw the man try to cover his face with his hands, only to have them knocked down so that all could see who he was.

"The walk of shame," a voice said behind Angeline. In French!

She whipped around to see Zeid standing behind her. Stephen was with him. Stephen seemed as astounded to see her as she was to see him.

"Punishment meted out by the muhtasib to a thief who has tried to cheat the people. Our muhtasib enforces the laws well here," Zeid said.

Angeline barely heard him. Samah made an exclamation of annoyance, but Zeid barked out a few short words and she was silenced. Samah's whole body went rigid with anger.

"Stephen!" Angeline cried, ignoring both Samah and Zeid. "I have been wanting to see you so much! How fare you?" To her delight, Stephen's face lit up, if only briefly, in a smile.

"I, too, am glad to see you!" he answered. "I am well . . . as well as can be expected," he corrected himself. The smile died and his eyes grew dull again.

Angeline could see an ugly, half-healed scar on his forehead. Stephen rubbed at it, then seemed to make an effort to regain his enthusiasm.

"But you," he said. "Zeid has told me that you are being well treated and that the concubine, Zahra, has grown fond of you."

Fond of her? Zahra had grown fond of her?

"She is good to me," she replied. "But everything is strange here, Stephen. I am so alone and I have worried about you. I miss you!"

"I have missed you, too," Stephen replied. He dropped his hand to his side and stood for a moment, hunched, as if cold, even though the sun beat down upon them with an unrelenting heat. "Zeid reassured me that you were not being mistreated . . ." He stopped, said nothing for a long moment, then drew a deep breath and spoke again.

"This is not how we thought it would end, is it, Angeline?"

Angeline's initial relief at seeing him died. She could not bear to see him so defeated, so hopeless. He looked hollow. Empty. Like a cast-off, burned up lantern.

Samah was tugging at her arm. Must she go back to the harem and not see him again? She could not!

As if sensing her thoughts, Stephen spoke quickly.

"I will see you again, Angeline." He drew another deep breath, as if summoning up strength, then turned back to Zeid.

"I work with Kareem the gardener in the mornings," he said, "but in the afternoons I help Father Martin when he teaches the Emir's son, Habib. If Father Martin sent for Angeline, would she be allowed to go to him? Our priest has worried about her. He worries that she is not hearing Mass. That she has not made her confession since we've been here."

Zeid nodded. "It could be done," he said. "The maid could come to Father Martin after Habib has finished."

Her patience exhausted, Samah snapped out a few words to Zeid and he nodded.

"Go with Samah now," he said to Angeline. "I will arrange it. You will be summoned when it is time." He smiled. There was even a flicker of what might have been amusement in his eyes. "You have a right to worship with your priest," he said, "and I do not think anyone would find it amiss if Stephen were there, too."

"Thank you," Angeline said. She felt suddenly light. "I will come if I am allowed, Stephen," she said. "We will be together again, you will see. Perhaps then we can bear this."

How strange, she thought. I am comforting him. When all the time we were on that terrible journey, it was he who comforted me.

Angeline waited impatiently for the call to go to Father Martin. Finally, one day after their afternoon sleep, Samah came for her, heavily veiled. Zahra must have been expecting her, because she was not surprised.

"Imshi," she said.

Angeline had heard the other concubines say that to the slave girls often enough to know that it meant *Off with you*. The other women snapped it out as a curt command, but Zahra said it almost affectionately. She waved Angeline out of the room.

Samah led Angeline through an unfamiliar part of the house, then they descended into a small garden at the back. Angeline thought she saw the whisk of a gown disappear into a doorway as they crossed to a separate wing of the residence. There they followed another passageway to the end. A door stood open and Angeline could hear Father Martin's voice. Samah led her up to the room, every stiff step expressing her disapproval. At the doorway she turned quickly and left.

When Angeline entered, she could not suppress the rush of gladness that overwhelmed her. Father Martin rose from where he had been sitting at a table and came toward her. She almost hugged him. Stephen stood behind the priest. She rushed over to him and held out her hands.

"Now we can really talk," she began.

Father Martin interrupted her. "I believed it was for religious instruction you wished these meetings?" His voice was dry but there was a smile behind the words. "I suggest we pray," he said.

Chastened, Angeline fell to her knees beside him. At first she wished only to be done with it and allowed to talk to Stephen but, as they prayed, she felt a quietness steal over her. After all this time of strange customs and ways, it was a solace to hear the familiar words. She found herself praying more earnestly and sincerely than ever before in her life. She prayed for herself, for all the others who had died on the crusade, for those whose fate was unknown to her—and for Stephen. But, to her dismay, she saw that Stephen did not pray.

Did he still believe that God had deserted him? Betrayed him? Had he been able to find no comfort at all in these last few weeks?

There was time for talk after the prayers. Father Martin moved to a small table in the middle of the room and began to prepare his lesson for the next day.

"I must make ready for Habib, the little prince," he said. "He has just left us for his daily lessons in the Qur'an."

"What is that?" Angeline asked.

"That is the holy book of the Muslims," he replied. "Every boy is required to memorize it."

"The entire book?" Angeline asked.

"The entire book," he confirmed.

"It must be very short then," she said, thinking of the thickness of the Holy Bible that the Christian priests read from.

"It is not," Father Martin answered. "I have seen it. It is as full a book as our True Book. A wonderful endeavour it is, that every boy should learn it all by memory. Or would be, if it were not heresy," he added quickly. "Would that our Christian children were required to do the same with the Word of God."

Angeline looked at him more closely. He was wearing the same cassock that he had worn all during their journey. Clean now, but mended to the point where there seemed to be more stitching than original cloth. Father Martin saw her look.

"They have allowed me to keep my own robes," he said. "They do respect our religion. I would not have believed it, but it is so."

"What do you teach Habib?" Angeline asked. She was intrigued in spite of her impatience to talk to Stephen.

"How to read and write in Latin," Father Martin replied. "And French. Stephen assists me, and in so doing," he added with a full smile this time, "he is learning also."

Angeline was incredulous. Stephen had been a shepherd boy. He had never been able to read. He hadn't even been able to read the letter that the mysterious stranger had given him. It had been Father Martin, the young priest from his village, who had read it for him.

"Can you read now?" she asked Stephen. "Can you write?"

"A little," Stephen admitted. "Only a little," he hastened to add.

Angeline was struck with a thought. If Stephen could learn to read and write, why not she?

"Could you teach me as well, Father?" she asked. "If they allow me to come here often, could you teach me?"

"I suppose . . ." Father Martin began. "But what use would you have of it? You are but a maid . . ."

Angeline bristled, but held back the angry retort that threatened to spill out. Instead, she said, "Zahra, the concubine who . . ." The words stuck in her throat. She forced herself to go on. "The concubine who owns me," she said, "can read and write. She copies the books the Emir brings home from the palace library. Wonderful books they are! Bound in the finest leather and with illuminations of real gold! Her copies are as fine as the originals. And she has taught me a few words in Arabic that I write as well . . ." She stopped, aware that Father Martin's face had frozen.

"A concubine?" he demanded. "Learned?"

"She is," Angeline replied. To her surprise, she found herself defending Zahra hotly. "She is a *very* learned woman."

"Why could we not do this?" Stephen broke in. "What harm is there in it?"

Angeline threw him a grateful glance.

Father Martin's face thawed. "It is good to have you here, my child," he said. "And to know that you are well, although I am dismayed by the sinful woman you are forced to serve. Lessons from the Bible would probably do you good."

Angeline flushed. At that moment Father Martin sounded much like Father Bertrand, who had condemned her mother so unfairly. Truly, although she had not thought on it before, her mother and Zahra were not so unalike. They were both women full of love and, most of all, love for their children. There were far worse in the world, as Angeline had the misfortune to know, even amongst those who were properly wed. But again, she held her tongue. It would do no good to anger Father Martin. She must not risk losing the precious opportunity to learn how to read and write.

She turned toward Stephen.

"What is your life like here?" she asked. "Are you well treated?"

Stephen grimaced.

"Well treated, yes. For a slave."

Angeline caught the bitterness underlying his words; nevertheless, she persisted.

"But tell me, what do you do? How do you pass your days?"

Stephen looked down at his hands. The left

one bore shiny scars. Stephen's father had not believed the letter to be from God and had thrown the parchment in the fire. Stephen had thrust his hand into the flames to save it. He rubbed at the scars now. It seemed he would not speak, but Father Martin prodded him.

"Tell her of your work with Kareem," he said.

"That old man!" Stephen exclaimed. "He has the most evil temper I have ever known."

"But he has taught you much about gardens and the growing of living plants, has he not?" Father Martin insisted.

"He has," Stephen answered, but he turned away. "It will be useful if I am to be a slave in this heathen land for the rest of my life, I suppose."

Angeline would not give up.

"Well, I will tell you about how I spend my time," she said, forcing a gaiety into her voice that she could not feel. She went on to describe her life with Zahra, exaggerating the luxury, embellishing every detail. Little by little, she managed to draw Stephen out, but when she tried to talk of their journey Stephen silenced her.

"I cannot speak of that," he said.

Samah returned before the evening prayer to take Angeline back to Zahra. Angeline fetched Zahra's meal, played with Aza for a while, then curled up on her couch. Zahra was not going to the Emir that night. Angeline lay in the darkness, staring out the window at the stars. There was much to think about. Suddenly her life had taken a new turn. A better turn, she hoped. Being able to see Stephen would help. But the thought of him was troubling. She remembered the look on his face while Father Martin prayed and he would not. It was a look of such pain and sorrow. He would not speak of their journey, but here in the silent darkness, Angeline could not help remembering.

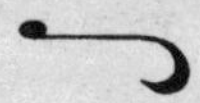

They had embarked in seven ships from Marseilles, Stephen once more alive with hope and faith after the shock of his failure to part the sea.

"God has answered our prayers in His own way!" he had cried. "Behold, our faith in Him has been answered. We *will* go to the Holy Land. We *will* restore Jerusalem to the true faith. God wills it! Those who deserted us will hear of our triumph and they will regret their faithlessness to their dying day."

Never would she forget the feeling of standing beside him on the heaving, rolling deck that first morning as they faced the east together, braced against the wind. The sun had shone down upon them; the waves danced and glittered. Seabirds swooped and called as the great ship's sails billowed and cracked above them. The oarsmen shipped their oars. They were on their way! Angeline had been filled with joy. Stephen's arm around her had been firm and strong.

Everything had seemed possible.

But then they had been crammed below decks and the hatch locked down. The ship had seemed huge to her, but even so there was not room enough for the hundreds of children who had been crowded into the hold. They were packed in so tightly there was barely room for each child to find a space to sit. Here below the deck, the motion of the ship was a horrible, rolling wallow that threw all of them against each other. It was not long before the children began to vomit . . .

She could not stop the memories that crowded into her mind now, one upon the other.

That night and the day after were the worst she had ever spent. Worse, even, than the most terrible day of their journey. They were given no food, no water. There was barely any light and no room at all to move around. The heat beat down on them in a smothering blanket. It was almost impossible to breathe. Children vomited continuously. Pots had been provided for them, but they were soon overflowing and most children just relieved themselves where they sat. To

Angeline's shame, she was in no better state than any of the others. Even Father Martin soiled himself. They avoided each other's eyes.

"At least we are on our way," Stephen had said, his faith still strong. "This will not last forever and, when it is over, we will have reached the Holy Land. We will have reached Jerusalem." He tried to preach, but the children were too sick to hear him.

Two days out of Marseilles a terrible storm struck. The ship began to roll even more wildly. Angeline could still hear the noise of the wind screaming in the sails. The waves battered against the side of the ship and filled her with terror. At any moment she had expected to see a breach open up in the hull and the water pour in through it. The children had been in even worse straits and she had forced herself to try to help them, but there was little she had been able to do. She had staggered from one to another, trying to reassure them, but they could not be comforted. Then she had found two who would not respond at all, and she realized they were dead. She had called to Father Martin to help. He said a blessing over their bodies, then he and Stephen managed to carry them to the foot of the ladder. Stephen beat on the hatch and called to the sailors, but there was no answer.

It was not until the morning of the fourth day

that the storm subsided. By then, three more children had died. When the hatch was finally raised, no one reacted for several moments, so stunned were they by the daylight and fresh air. A sailor's face had appeared at the opening, grimacing at the stink that rose to greet him.

"There are dead children down here," Stephen called. "You must send someone down to take them up."

"Bring them yourselves," the sailor yelled back. His face disappeared.

Stephen had dragged himself to his feet and lifted one of the bodies. Angeline summoned what little strength she had left and bent to help Father Martin with another. Between them, they carried the dead up to the deck and gave them into the care of the sailors. To Angeline's horror, the sailors took hold of the small bodies and hurled them overboard one by one.

Then Stephen had looked around at the still-angry sea.

"I count only four other ships," he cried. The wind was strong and it snatched his words away. "There are two missing!"

"Foundered in the storm, they did," a sailor yelled back. "On the rocks of San Pietro. It was only by the grace of God that we did not follow them."

Angeline turned away from the stars shining so steadily through the window. She buried her face in her pillow.

God's grace had saved them from drowning—but not to set Jerusalem free. They had been saved instead to be brought to Egypt. To where the slave traders awaited them.

"We cannot question God's purpose," Father Martin had said.

But Stephen did.

And she?

She did not know.

Chapter Eight

Angeline could not be certain that she would be allowed to return to Father Martin, but she waited impatiently all the next week, hoping that she would. So eager was she to see Stephen again and start learning to read and write that she could almost ignore Anka when the girl deliberately tripped her on the way back to the harem from the cooking place. She managed to regain her balance without dropping the tray she carried for Zahra, and contented herself with throwing Anka a withering glance. Perhaps, she thought, she could ask Stephen to find out some swear words in Arabic for her to use on the pestilential girl. Surely the gardener must swear a lot—Stephen had said he was bad-tempered and he certainly looked it. She smiled at the thought, but Nabeela, who was tittering behind Anka, believed her to be mocking them and took offence. She reached out and pinched Angeline hard on the arm. This time Angeline nearly did drop the tray. Angered now, she aimed a kick at the girl, but Nabeela avoided it easily. Angeline glared after her.

Zahra raised her eyebrows at the scowl on Angeline's face when she finally managed to get the tray of juice and sweetmeats to her. She asked a question, but Angeline just shook her head and forced her features into a blank expression. There was no use complaining to Zahra about the girls, even if she could.

She went about her duties in a fever of anticipation for the next week. Then, one day when the afternoon rest was over, Samah returned, heavily veiled again and exuding, if possible, even more disapproval. Angeline leaped up from where she had been mending a scarf of Zahra's—she may have hated sewing when she was younger, but the skill was useful to her now. She was at Samah's side in an instant, only barely remembering to look to Zahra for permission to leave.

They took the same route through the small garden at the back of the house. This time Angeline clearly saw a woman disappear into the doorway. The woman paused to glance back over her shoulder. She caught Angeline's eyes and held them for the briefest of moments, then she melted into the shadows beyond. Samah saw the woman at the same time and, with a hiss of fright, she pulled Angeline back and held her there until the woman was gone. Angeline was instantly curious. Who was this woman and why was Samah so fearful of intruding on her privacy? She must be a person of great importance, Angeline thought, then she pushed the matter out of her mind in her hurry to get to Father Martin.

"I'm back!" she exclaimed as she entered the classroom, then she stopped short. Father Martin and Stephen sat at the table, but a young boy was there also. He was in the process of gathering up some books and writing materials. He was small and very slim, dressed in a rich, shimmering green robe. He wore soft leather boots and a gold-coloured turban. Angeline noticed his hands especially—he had fine, long-boned, graceful fingers. He drew himself up with a haughty air when he saw Angeline and stared at her with disapproval, but Angeline could believe that she saw interest there as well.

"Qui es-tu?" he demanded in a strangely accented French. *Who are you?*

This must be the young prince, Habib. Father Martin had said that he was only nine years old but she panicked for a moment. Young or not, he was a prince. Should she curtsy?

"Angeline," she replied. "Your Highness," she added quickly. Was that the proper way to address him? She made a quick sort of bob, but her foot tangled in her long skirt and she stumbled. She thought she saw the prince's mouth twitch with a quickly suppressed smile. Without thinking, she smiled back. Instantly, his face fell back into an arrogant stare. He wheeled around and left the room by a doorway that led into a different part of the house from the women's. Samah was sputtering behind her, then she too turned and almost ran from the room.

For the rest of that afternoon, Angeline worked with Stephen and Father Martin. She was amazed at how much Stephen had learned already, and pleased to see that the work brought him out of his sorrow a bit. She was determined to catch up to him.

"Enough for today," Father Martin finally said, as the sun's rays slanted low into the room. "You have done well, my child."

Angeline sat back and sighed. Her head felt stuffed with new information, new thoughts.

"Does Habib learn quickly?" she asked.

"He does," Father Martin replied. "But Stephen even more so."

Angeline cast a sideways glance at Stephen. He had not spoken much, but seemed more at ease today, even though he had still not joined in the prayers. He, too, leaned back and stretched. She could believe that Stephen learned quickly. He had begun the crusade as an ignorant shepherd boy, but he had quickly learned the ways of leadership and power. Too well, she had sometimes thought. He had not been loathe to take on the trappings of a leader—riding in a banner-strewn cart while the others walked, and surrounding himself with the noblest of the boys who had joined them. Two of them, clad in mail and bearing swords, had ridden one on either side of him on magnificent horses. They were sons of one of France's most noble families and Stephen had been mightily proud of them. They had been amongst the first to desert him when the sea did not part at Marseilles, of course.

"Habib is a bright boy," Father Martin continued, "but a wilful child. He is too used to having his every wish granted, I think."

"He is still young," Angeline said. She could not help thinking of Marc and Yves. They had not been privileged as was Habib, but they, too, had been headstrong little boys. The memory was painful, however. She pushed it away.

"Am I to be allowed to come every week?" she asked instead.

"You are," Father Martin replied. "Zeid has arranged it."

"He seems a good man," Angeline said. "I wonder where he comes from?"

"He comes from a land far to the south of here," Stephen answered.

Angeline looked at him in surprise.

"He was captured in a raid when he was very young and brought here as a slave," Stephen went on. "He served the Emir all his life and was finally made steward."

"He is a slave?" Angeline asked, incredulous. She could not imagine such a dignified man being a slave.

"He was. The Emir gave him his freedom and allowed him to marry some years ago when he converted to Islam."

"He is wed?" Angeline asked again. Somehow she had not thought of Zeid as having any life of his own.

"He is wed and has four sons," Stephen answered. "I have met them. The eldest is almost my age."

"Are they slaves as well?" Angeline persisted, her curiosity in full bloom. She had not yet determined who in this household were slaves and who were servants.

"No, they are not. They were born after he was freed. The eldest is being educated to be a secretary to the Emir."

"But how is it that Zeid speaks French?" Angeline asked.

"He was not much more than a babe when he was captured and brought here," Stephen said. "Another slave took him under her care and nursed him until he was old enough to fend for himself. She was French. She had been captured in a raid on a French merchant ship."

"She must have been Christian then!" Angeline exclaimed. "Perhaps that is why he has been so kind to us. Do you know what happened to her?"

"She died, Zeid told me," Stephen replied. "He sorrowed for her as much as for a mother. Indeed, she was the only mother he ever knew."

At that moment Samah appeared. Angeline followed her back to Zahra's room, mulling over Stephen's words. It was hard for her to believe that Zeid had been a slave.

From such a harsh beginning, he has done well for himself, she thought.

Zahra was generous and often allowed Angeline, accompanied by Samah, to go to Father Martin after she had finished her day's work. On those days Zahra would put her quill down with a sigh of relief, stretch, and call Aza to her, then she would take Aza to a small secluded garden at the back of the concubines' quarters to play. Angeline had caught sight of them once when she was fetching some food from the cooking place and, her mind on other things, she had taken a wrong turn. Zahra had been chasing the child in and out of the bushes and laughing as if she were a child herself. Angeline had not been able to resist stopping to watch them. But when a cat, angry at having its peace disturbed, streaked by and Aza seemed as if she would chase after it, Angeline drew quickly back out of sight and hurried off to complete her errand. It was a private moment—Zahra would not want her intruding upon it, she was sure.

Sometimes during their afternoons with Father Martin, Stephen talked and worked with Angeline. Other days he sat by the window, sunk in gloom, and would not speak at all. Nor would he ever join in Father Martin's prayers. One day, to Angeline's consternation, he was not there.

"Where is Stephen?" she asked when she entered the room.

"Kareem said he had need of him today," Father Martin answered. "It is not a Christian thing to say, but I think the old man is jealous of the time Stephen spends here with the young prince and invents tasks for Stephen in order to keep him away."

Disappointed, Angeline settled to her work, but after only a few moments she laid her quill down.

"What is it?" Father Martin asked. "Are you not well?"

"No—I am well enough," she answered, "but I worry about Stephen. What can I do to help him, Father? I cannot bear to see him so anguished."

Father Martin stroked the tattered cover of the Bible from which he had been reading. He rubbed his forehead with his other hand.

"I know not what you can do, my child. I have tried without success to give him comfort. It pains me, as well, to see him so tormented. I am certain our good Lord means not for him to suffer so. He acted only in faith. If he was misled—if I and all the others were misled—it was only through our belief that God had truly spoken to us through the Christ Himself." He stopped and closed his eyes for a moment. His lips moved in silent prayer.

Angeline bit her lip. "Will he recover, Father?" she asked. It was little more than a whisper.

"I know not," the priest replied. "We must trust in God."

I *will* trust in God, Angeline thought, but I will also try by every means *I* can to help him.

She missed the vibrant and forceful boy she had known and come to care for so deeply. She missed *Stephen*.

After a few weeks Angeline was allowed to go see Father Martin and return by herself. It seemed that she had regained Zahra's confidence, and she resolved not to do anything to lose that trust again. It still surprised her how much Zahra's loss of faith in her had troubled her. And it had frightened her.

I am not a child anymore, she thought. There is no one here to take care of me as my mother did. Certainly Zahra, kind though she may be, will not. I must tread carefully here. I must take care of *myself*.

She was, however, becoming more and more intrigued by the mysterious woman she kept catching glimpses of in the small garden on her way to Father Martin's classroom. Could it be that the woman waited for her on purpose? It almost seemed so, but what could that purpose be, and why did she not make herself known to Angeline? Who was she? Angeline had seen enough of her to realize that she was dressed as finely as Zahra, if not more so, and she was veiled, but she could not be a concubine. The concubines were not allowed out of the harem.

Another oddity. Several times Habib was still with Father Martin when she arrived. He had not spoken to her again, but every time she saw him he seemed to look at her with more curiosity.

"I believe he tarries on purpose to see you," Father Martin said with a smile one day. "I think him to be fascinated with you. Aside from his sisters, you are probably the only girl he has ever met. And I am certain that you are different indeed from them."

"How many sisters does he have?" Angeline asked. She was as interested in the little prince as he was in her.

"Several," Father Martin answered. "Habib is the eldest son of the Emir's youngest wife." His mouth quirked with disapproval when he spoke the word "youngest." "He has two brothers, one a mere babe in arms, the other not much older. The Emir's other wives have only daughters. I know not how many."

"How many wives does the Emir have?" Angeline asked, astounded.

"Three. It is the custom here to have several." The tone of his voice left no doubt as to what he thought about that.

Three, Angeline thought. And many concubines. Father Bertrand would have perished from the shock of it! She could not suppress a small, secret smile but she hid it from Father Martin.

Then one day, to Angeline's surprise, when she entered the garden the mysterious woman was sitting on a bench and did not dart away.

"Taaly huna ya bint," she said, and beckoned to Angeline. *Come here, girl.* Angeline knew enough Arabic by now to understand that phrase.

Stunned, and not a little apprehensive, she approached the woman cautiously.

The woman said a few words more. Angeline stood helplessly in front of her.

"Ana mish fahema," she faltered. *I don't understand.* That was a phrase she had learned early on and had need of often.

"Ismi Nusaybah," the woman said. *My name is Nusaybah.* That much Angeline could also understand. But then she added, "Ana umu Habib."

Angeline could make out the word "ana," which meant I, and the name, Habib. Then she caught her breath. Could she be saying "I am Habib's mother?"

Nusaybah spoke again. Her voice was soft and

lilting, but overlaid with sadness. Angeline could only shake her head helplessly. Nusaybah's words meant nothing to her.

Nusaybah realized that Angeline could not understand her; she stopped speaking. She stood, reached out a bejewelled hand, and gave Angeline's arm a light pat. Then she turned and made her way inside the house.

She *was* Habib's mother. She had exactly the same fine, slim hands as he.

Angeline burst into the classroom.

"I saw Habib's mother!" she cried, then stopped short as she noticed the prince sitting at the table next to Stephen.

The boy's head jerked up. He stared at her, his eyes suddenly bright.

"Ma mère?" he demanded. "You saw my mother?" Then he caught himself, embarrassed, and a flush stained his dark cheeks.

"Je m'excuse." He rose quickly, trying to recover his dignity. "Excuse me, it is late. I must be going." He scrambled his papers together and almost ran out of the room.

Angeline stared after him, open-mouthed. She turned a questioning look on Father Martin.

"He has not seen his mother for some time," Father Martin explained. "He is too old now to live in the women's quarters—he lives with his father."

"Does he not visit her?" Angeline asked, incredulous.

"No. He is allowed to, but he is a prideful boy and feels that it shows weakness."

"So that is why she waits for me," Angeline said. "She must know that I see him every week. She must have been asking me about him."

If only I could talk to her, she thought. And with that thought came a determination. I know a few words of their language already, she told herself. I'll learn more. Zahra will teach me. I'll learn enough so that I *can* talk to her.

And perhaps I can do something to change Habib's mind, as well, she thought. I will have to be wary. He waits for me to come, but he does not like it if I speak to him. She mulled the problem over for a moment, then suppressed a sly smile.

There is nothing to stop me from saying what I wish to Stephen and Father Martin, she thought, and would it be my fault if he overheard me? No boy should slight his mother so—not even a prince.

The next day Nusaybah was sitting on her bench as usual when Angeline crossed the garden. She waved Angeline over to her, but did not speak. Instead, she contented herself by patting Angeline on the arm again, then she rose to leave. As she walked away, Angeline heard her sigh.

When Angeline entered the classroom, Habib was still there, but almost immediately he gathered up his books and started to leave. Angeline sat down at the table and made a great show of settling to her work.

"I saw the prince's mother again today," she said to Stephen in an offhand manner, as if the words were of no importance at all. "She seemed so sad. I think she might have been weeping."

Habib made no indication that he had heard her, but out of the corner of her eye, she saw him hesitate for a brief moment before going out the door.

As they worked together that afternoon, Angeline found herself distracted. For some reason she could not concentrate on her tasks. Beside her, Stephen bent over his papers, his brow furrowed with concentration. She could smell the faint aura of his sweat. It was familiar to her. She realized that she would be able to recognize Stephen anywhere, even if blindfolded, by that smell.

On the crusade they had forged a bond, but friendship it had been, no more. How could it have been otherwise? Stephen's passion had, indeed, been all for his mission. He could think of nothing else. And she had thought of him only as their leader. But now? She saw the line of his jaw, the set of his mouth, so fierce and determined. A stray lock of hair fell into his eyes. Without meaning to, she reached out to brush it away. Then she realized what she was doing and drew her hand back, shocked. To her relief, Stephen had not noticed.

Whatever had possessed her to do such a thing?

Chapter Nine

One morning Angeline awoke to find a light rain falling. She realized that it was the first time it had rained in the months since she had arrived in Egypt. When Zahra arose from her bed she shivered and asked Angeline to fetch her a light woolen shawl.

"It is so cold," Zahra complained, but to Angeline it seemed as if the weather were just finally becoming bearable.

Angeline's efforts to learn the language were succeeding. She was understanding more and more of what people were saying to her and that helped to make life a little easier. When she and Samah went to the suq now, she could often pick out words from the babble surrounding her. Zahra encouraged her and was a patient teacher. Angeline, on her part, enjoyed forming the strange symbols and learning what they meant.

Angeline learned from Aza, too. Mostly the words for sweetmeats or treats, but once a word that Aza was punished for saying. Shocked, Zahra had forbade the child any cakes for a week. It must have been a very bad word that Aza had overheard somewhere, probably in the cooking place, but Angeline had no idea what it meant. She tucked it away in her mind to use on Anka and the other vexatious girls the next time they tormented her.

Angeline's lessons with Father Martin were also going on apace. Habib was usually there when she arrived and she often managed to speak of Nusaybah within his hearing. He never made any sign that he had heard, but she noticed that he was getting slower and slower to leave every day. Angeline waited. One day, surely, he would ask about his mother.

The next time she saw Nusaybah sitting on her bench, on an impulse, Angeline crossed over to her and without permission, sat beside her.

"Ibn habdritik bekhier wa saeed," she said, haltingly, searching for the words with difficulty but determined to speak. *Your son is well and happy.*

Nusaybah responded with a torrent of words, none of which Angeline understood, but she had no trouble hearing the longing in the woman's voice. She made certain to report it to Father Martin in Habib's hearing.

Finally the day came when Angeline entered the classroom to find Father Martin beaming. Habib, too, seemed happier and more lively than Angeline had yet seen him.

"The prince has asked to see his mother," the priest announced as soon as Habib was out of the room. "I am relieved that the poor woman will have some comfort."

The following week, Nusaybah rose and embraced Angeline the moment she set foot in the garden.

"Shukran, binty," she said. *Thank you, my little one.*

Angeline felt very pleased with herself. And Father Martin had expressed sympathy for Nusaybah—a third wife! Could it be that he was becoming more tolerant?

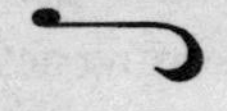

Angeline's days were full and busy; there were times when she almost forgot she was a slave. Stephen, however, seemed to be sinking further and further into despair. Rarely now did he smile. Angeline found herself growing impatient.

"Stephen, did you not tell me that King Philip himself thought you had been deluded by some priest?" she demanded one afternoon when Father Martin, who was feeling ill, had left. Stephen had been so depressed that he had not joined in their work at all, and Angeline was exasperated with him in spite of herself.

He did not answer, would not even look at her, only stood staring out the window.

"If so," Angeline insisted, "and even if that priest *meant* well, the guilt lies with him, not with you. Father Martin has said that you have only to make your confession to him and God will forgive you."

At that, Stephen whipped around to face her.

"Can you not understand?" he burst out with such sudden violence that Angeline drew back, shocked. "Can you not understand?" he repeated. "I do not *want* God's forgiveness! God abandoned me and all those who followed me. What I want is the forgiveness of those whom I led to death or slavery, and that is impossible. You, Angeline . . . How can *you* forgive me?"

"There is nothing for me to forgive," Angeline answered. Her voice shook. "I followed you of my own free will," she said. "As did all of the others."

"But I failed you." Stephen's voice broke. He reached out and took Angeline's face in his hands. "It is my fault that you are here—that you are a slave. You, who stayed by me when so many others abandoned me. When I look at you I cannot bear what I have done to you."

"Yes, I stayed by you." Angeline's face burned with the heat from his hands. "And I will stay by you here, too, if you will but let me."

Stephen dropped his hands. "I am not worthy," he said. He turned and, before Angeline could stop him, left the room.

The next morning Zahra gave Angeline to understand that she and Samah were to take Aza with them to the suq. At least, that was what Angeline thought. But when they left, with Samah heavily veiled as usual, they did not take the now-familiar route to the market. Instead, they wound their way through different streets until they reached a small mosque. Angeline followed Samah warily. She had no idea what this meant. Aza, however, seemed excited and bounded along beside them, babbling all the while.

Samah led the way around to the back of the mosque. There, in an enclosed courtyard, were assembled several other girls of about Aza's age. A robed man sat on a platform in front of them. Samah gestured to Angeline to wait while she took Aza up to him. She exchanged some words with the man, then Aza, never one for shyness, plopped herself down eagerly in the very front row. The man began to speak and Angeline realized that he was a teacher. This was a school for girls—probably for daughters of the servants and slaves who lived in the neighbourhood. Samah and Angeline left Aza there and went to do some errands at the suq. They returned to fetch her after an hour or so.

They followed this pattern nearly every day from then on, either filling the time while Aza learned by going to the suq, or just sitting outside the mosque, waiting. Finally, Zahra gave orders that Angeline should take Aza on her own.

One day, when Zahra did not have any errands for her to run, Angeline decided to use her free time to explore a bit. She was comfortable enough by now with the city and with the language to walk by herself, and Zahra had allowed her the freedom. As a young slave girl she was largely ignored, but never in any danger. She ambled aimlessly amongst the crowds for a while, then turned down a cobbled street that looked quiet and cool. There were houses along this street, with second-floor balconies enclosed by wooden screens. Once she heard giggles coming from behind one and she caught a flash of brilliant material through the lattice-work. Her lips twisted in a wry smile. Well-born ladies, no doubt, such as the Emir's wives, peeking through to observe the street activity. Women who could not go out unveiled or without attendants. Being a slave did have its compensations. Then she swore as she stepped in a puddle of filth—that word Aza had been punished for saying did have its uses—and began to pay more attention to where she was placing her feet.

The street made a sharp turn and she followed it. At the end, she saw a church. A Christian church! Its cross stood out tall against the sky. Intrigued, she drew near to it. The door stood open and the interior beckoned, dark and cool; silent—no Mass was being said at that time. She tiptoed in, then stopped, awestruck. This was not like any church she had ever seen before. The church of her village was small and rough, with a crude altar and rushes on a dirt floor. She supposed that the great cathedrals of the cities they had passed through in France must have been wondrous, too, but she had had no opportunity to enter them. Here, in this church, the ceilings arched high above her, supported by pillars sheathed in gold that glimmered in the light of many candles. The floor was paved with smooth stones. In the centre of the church stood a massive pulpit made of intricately carved wood and lavishly decorated. Paintings of Jesus covered one wall, more paintings hung on the others. She stood, lost in wonder, then jumped as a figure who had been kneeling at the side of the pulpit rose to his feet. She had not noticed him there. It was a boy about Stephen's age. He asked a question in a tongue she could not understand. When she shook her head helplessly, he repeated the question in Arabic.

"Mun unti? Ma dha tuf ali huna?" *Who are you? What are you doing here?*

He did not sound angry or annoyed that she had interrupted him, just curious.

"Ismi Angeline," she replied tentatively.

"Are you a slave?" he asked.

"I am," she replied. "I am Zahra's slave, in the house of the Emir Abd'al Haseeb." She searched for the correct words with difficulty but he seemed to understand her.

He looked at her closely. "You are not Arab," he said.

"No, I am a Christian," she replied. "From the Frankish lands."

"Ah, a Franj," he said, peering at her with more interest. "I have heard much of you people. "None of it good," he added.

"Why not?" Angeline asked, not certain she had understood the boy correctly. "Ismak eh?" *What is your name?*

"Ibrahim," he answered. "I am Christian, too. But I am Egyptian. A true Egyptian. We Copts are the only people in Egypt who are descended from the ancients."

Angeline's head was swimming. She could make no sense of this. At that moment she realized that it would most certainly be time for Aza to finish her lesson. She could not be late. In a panic she blurted out, "I have to go. Ma'as salama!" *Goodbye!* Then she turned and ran.

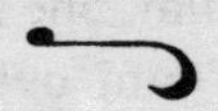

The next time she met with Father Martin she was full of questions.

"These Egyptian Christians," she burst out. "How are they different? Why do they dislike the Frankish people?"

Father Martin made the same sour face that

he had made when they had seen the Christian riding through the street the day they arrived.

"They are Coptic Christians," he repeated. Seeing that Angeline still looked puzzled, he explained. "We in the Western world believe the Copts to be misguided," he said. "Misguided to the point of heresy. They do not believe in the dual nature of our Lord Jesus. They acknowledge him to be Divine only, and not a man as well. They ignore all who try to bring them back to the true religion. Their churches here are not true Christian churches at all."

Angeline felt it might be best not to mention that she had been in one of those churches and had spoken to one of those Copts, but she saw Stephen looking at her. She determined to tell him of her meeting with Ibrahim at the first opportunity. Perhaps this might be something that would interest him. She would grasp at any opportunity to pull him out of the grief that seemed to weigh him down so implacably.

The opportunity came that very afternoon. Father Martin again declared himself to be feeling unwell and retired early to his room. Angeline wondered briefly if he were annoyed with her questions and only seeking an excuse to take himself away, but the priest did seem pale and tired.

When Father Martin had left, however, Angeline found herself suddenly shy. She and Stephen had not been alone since the afternoon of Stephen's outburst—there had been an awkwardness between them ever since. Stupidly, she found herself flushing at the memory of the touch of his hands upon her face. She turned away to hide her flaming cheeks. It seemed as if Stephen, too, felt ill at ease. They both fell silent. Then, to Angeline's relief, he spoke.

"Why were you asking about the Egyptian Christians?" he asked. "How do you know they do not like the Franks?"

Angeline turned back eagerly. This she could talk about.

"I met one!" she answered. "A boy. About our age. His name is Ibrahim. He told me that the Copts don't like the Franks, but he did not seem to dislike *me*."

"But where did you meet him?" Stephen asked. "How?"

"At a church," Angeline replied. "A Christian church. A Coptic Christian church I suppose it must be, but it was glorious, Stephen! So beautiful!" She rushed on. "I have never seen anything like it before. I cannot believe such a church to be as dreadful as Father Martin feels it to be. I take Zahra's daughter, Aza, to her lessons every morning. While she is there I sometimes wander the city. One day I found this church and Ibrahim was there." A sudden thought struck her. What if she were to arrange for Stephen to meet Ibrahim? Might that not help him?

"I go in the mornings," she said. "Would you like to go with me one day?"

"I work in the garden with Kareem at that time," Stephen answered. "It would not be possible." He shrugged. "It is of no interest to me in any case." He turned back to his work.

Angeline grew silent but she was not about to give up. She would grasp at anything that might spark Stephen's curiosity. Father Martin would surely disapprove, of course, but he need know nothing about it. If it would help Stephen . . .

Angeline determined to go back to the church as soon as possible, but Zahra kept her busy with errands for the next few days and she had no time. Then Aza had a holiday from her lessons, and they resumed their mornings in the harem. One day, while Angeline was helping Zahra dress, Zahra began to talk about her past.

"I was no older than you, binty," she said, "when I was sold to the Emir as a concubine. My family thought it great good fortune for me. I was one of his favourites right from the beginning, but I was not happy here. I was frightened. Just as you were when you first arrived."

Angeline started to shake her head in fierce denial.

"Oh yes you were, binty. You could not hide it." She went on. "It was Samah who took care of me then and comforted me." She laughed at the disbelieving expression on Angeline's face.

"Yes, Samah. She has a good heart, but she keeps it well hidden."

Zahra waved Angeline aside and walked over to the window. She stared out at the garden below, then turned back to Angeline.

"When Samah finally got me to stop feeling sorry for myself, I began to think about how I could better my life here. I asked the Emir if I could be tutored in the art of copying and he agreed. That was how I learned to read and write. And that was how I made myself more important than those other useless women in the harem," she said with a sly smile. Then she added, "You will find your place here too, binty. I am certain of it."

Angeline did not answer. She busied herself with tidying up, but her thoughts were on what Zahra had told her. Zahra had once been as lonely and frightened as she. Zahra understood how she felt and was trying to be as kind to

Angeline as Samah had been to her. Angeline could not believe that she would ever fit in here, but, for the first time, she felt something that was almost gratitude toward the concubine.

The next morning, Angeline was secretly pleased to see Zahra gather up some of her work to take to the harem. She felt a surge of pride that Zahra thought it good enough to show to the other women. When they reached the harem, she could hear sprightly music being played. Anka and the other three girls were dancing.

"They have been going to a dancing school for slave girls," Zahra whispered. "And very vain about it they are, too."

Angeline suspected that Zahra knew well what a trial those girls were to her. She had the words now to complain, but still she would not. It was a matter of pride. To her annoyance, the girls danced gracefully and beautifully—it made her feel large and clumsy just to watch them. When they finished, the women applauded and made what Angeline considered to be a very exaggerated and unwarranted fuss over them.

"Heba is to dance for the Emir himself," the woman reclining next to Zahra announced. "It is a great honour. It might even lead to her being chosen as a concubine! What good fortune that would be for her!"

The words were flattering, but the tone beneath them was spiteful. Angeline remembered Zahra calling them "useless women" the day before. The concubines led lives of pampered luxury, but they were still jealous of each other.

The dancing over, Zahra began to show the women the writing that Angeline had done.

"Has my little slave not learned well?" she asked.

Now it was Angeline's turn to smile. Perhaps Zahra was not as far above all the competition between the women as she had claimed. Zahra was obviously showing off her talents as a teacher as well as Angeline's progress as her student. Then Angeline saw Zahra pull out yet another piece of paper and, to her horror, she realized it was the drawing she had made of Anka, Heba, Nabeela, and Raful. Somehow it had gotten mixed in with the others.

Zahra had not seen it before and she looked at it with astonishment, then burst into laughter as she handed it around. The woman who had praised Heba so falsely was quick to call to the slave girl and hand the drawing to her. The other three crowded to look as well. As the concubines laughed, the four turned to glare at Angeline.

There was pure hate in their looks. Angeline stared back with all the arrogance she could muster, but her heart sank. They would have their revenge on her, she knew it.

But she couldn't help noticing that, in their fury, they looked exactly as she had drawn them.

Chapter Ten

"Zahra has told me that there are to be great festivities tonight here in Cairo for our Christian celebration of Epiphany," Angeline announced one day. "We will be able to observe the Feast of the Three Kings!"

Father Martin scowled. "They regard our holy festivals as no more than an excuse for gaiety," he said. "It is not a true celebration."

Angeline made a face behind his back. She had thought he might be pleased. It seemed to her that the priest was growing more short-tempered every day.

"Nevertheless, we are going to take part in it," she said. "Zahra has promised me."

"I will not," Father Martin growled. "Nor will Stephen. We will observe it quietly as we did Christmas these twelve days past."

"I do not wish to, in any case," Stephen said quickly.

But, for just a moment, Angeline was certain she saw a look cross his face that might have been disappointment. It gave her courage. Perhaps there was hope for him yet—and she was going to enjoy the festivities despite Father Martin's disapproval.

That night Zahra bundled up in her warmest shawl. Then she rummaged in a chest that stood beside her bed and came up with another shawl. She held it out to Angeline.

"Dah ashaanik ya binty," she said. *For you, my little one.*

Angeline reached out for it. It was made of the finest wool, a blue as clear as the Egyptian sky, shot through with golden threads. It felt so light it was as if she were holding a cloud. Never had she owned anything so fine.

"For me?" she asked, unable to believe Zahra meant it as a gift.

Zahra nodded.

"Shukran," Angeline whispered. "Shukran, Setti." She was so overcome she did not even realize that she had called Zahra "my Mistress" for the very first time.

After the evening prayer, they made ready. The days of this Egyptian winter seemed spring-like to Angeline, but the nights were even colder than they had been in the hot months. Angeline drew her shawl tightly around her shoulders as Zahra led her down through the house. To Angeline's surprise, they did not leave from the front but went instead through the small, jasmine-scented garden at the back. Instinctively, Angeline looked for Nusaybah, but she was nowhere to be seen. A servant waited to open a vine-covered door in the back wall that Angeline had not noticed before. On the other side a curtained litter filled with cushions and furs waited for them. They would be carried by the strongest of the Emir's slaves. Aza had been put to bed in the care of Samah, wailing because she could not go. Zahra's cheeks were flushed and her eyes bright with excitement. Angeline realized that this outing was a special treat for her. Again, Angeline reflected that being a slave did have advantages. Never would *she* wish to be a concubine.

They were carried down to the banks of the Nile River. Angeline peered out from behind the curtains.

"All of Cairo must be here!" she exclaimed.

Zahra, face veiled, peered out beside her.

"So many people!" she said.

Music filled the air. Men and women, too, were dancing. Angeline felt her own body sway in time with it. Food stalls were set up. The smells were enticing.

"Let me go and get something for us," Angeline begged. Truth to tell she was not so much hungry as eager to get out and be part of the festivities, but Zahra would not allow it.

"It would not be fitting."

"I could wear a veil," Angeline persisted. "I wouldn't mind."

"Not even then," Zahra replied. The tone of her voice brooked no argument, but Angeline took no note of it.

"Are you not hungry?" she demanded. In her eagerness she spoke more freely than she ever had. She caught herself and looked at Zahra warily, but Zahra seemed in too bright a mood to notice.

"You will get food, never fear," she said.

The slaves lowered the litter to the ground and Zahra leaned out to snap her fingers at one of them. She gave a quick order and the slave disappeared into the crowd, only to reappear with hot lamb sausages wrapped in palm leaves, dumplings filled with cheese, and a grilled vegetable that Angeline was growing fond of, called eggplant. It was dripping with the oil of olives and fragrant with spices. Another slave brought oranges and dates. Zahra spread the feast out between them in the litter.

"Bismillah ar-Rahman ar-Raheem," she murmured. The Muslim prayer before eating. *In the name of God, the Merciful, the Mercy-Giving.* She began to eat.

Angeline sat back, used to waiting until Zahra had finished, but Zahra would have none of that.

"Eat now," she said. "Eat with me tonight."

Angeline did not need a second invitation. She dipped her fingers into the eggplant willingly.

As they dined, they watched the revelry around them. On the shores of the Nile great torches flamed into the night. By their light, men and women ate and drank at the stalls. Musicians played music that had seemed strange to Angeline when she first came to Egypt, but which she now loved. People danced, her body swayed in time with them.

At one point, Angeline was certain she saw Ibrahim. He was with a tall man, richly dressed. His father perhaps? She renewed her resolve to find a way to introduce Stephen to him.

During the next few weeks she managed to return to the church a few times, but she did not see Ibrahim again. The church itself drew her, however, and she found herself looking forward to a few moments of peaceful prayer within whenever she was able to manage it. Although she was never there during Mass, once or twice she did catch sight of the Coptic Christian priest. He was a tall, formidable-looking man and Angeline was much too frightened to even think of approaching him. He wore a long white robe and was heavily bearded. She never mentioned these visits to Father Martin, knowing he would disapprove, but she did tell Stephen about them whenever she had the chance to speak to him out of the priest's hearing. She was certain that, in spite of himself, he was becoming interested.

"Have you never again seen that boy, Ibrahim?" he asked one day after she had described a baptism she had witnessed there.

"No," Angeline replied. "But I keep hoping I will."

And then, the very next week, she did see Ibrahim again. She had left Aza at her school and wandered over to the church. No sooner had she entered its dim stillness than she heard her name whispered.

"Angeline!"

She turned to see Ibrahim kneeling in one of the back pews. He rose and came toward her.

"I have been hoping that we would meet again," he said.

Together, they made their way out and sat on the low wall that surrounded the churchyard.

"Now," Ibrahim said. "Tell me about yourself. How did you, a Franj, come to be a slave in the Emir Abd'al Haseeb's house?

"It is a very long tale," Angeline said dubiously.

"Good," Ibrahim replied. "I love long tales. Begin!"

"Are you really interested?" Angeline asked, stalling a little. She had no idea where to start.

"I am," Ibrahim said.

She bit her lip, still hesitant, but Ibrahim was looking at her with such friendly, lively curiosity that she was encouraged.

"My mother died . . ." The words came slowly at first, but then more and more quickly. Ibrahim was a good listener. He interrupted her now and then with questions, but they only showed his interest. Angeline could not believe that he was so easy to talk to. As she spoke, it was as if a dam were released within her. A flood of words. When she had finished, they sat silent for a moment, then Ibrahim spoke.

"Your friend, this Stephen, how fares he now?

It must be hard for him, to lose such a dream. He must suffer terribly. Still, I cannot see that it was his fault."

"Nor can I," Angeline replied. "Our priest, Father Martin, believes now that it was another priest who tricked him. A priest who wanted the crusades to resume. Even our own King Philip of France thought that. He told Stephen to go home. To go back to his sheep."

She looked up at the sun which was high overhead.

"I must go now," she said. "It is time for Aza's class to be over."

"But you will come again?" Ibrahim asked.

"I will," Angeline answered.

"Good," Ibrahim said. "I have enjoyed listening to you."

"I have enjoyed talking to you," Angeline said. As she made her way back to the mosque she walked with a lighter step than ever before. How good it had been to tell everything! It was almost as if in the telling she had been able to rid herself of a heavy, heavy burden.

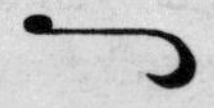

It was nearing the end of January and the beginning of the Muslim month of Ramadan.

"During Ramadan we do not eat or drink anything at all from sunrise to sunset," Zahra told her. "Fasting makes us disciplined. It trains us to endure hardship. Children are excepted, so Aza can eat, but those over fifteen years must fast. You are not Muslim; you may eat if you wish."

"I will fast," Angeline said. She could not explain even to herself why she wished to do this, but she did. Certainly neither Father Martin nor Stephen did so.

By late afternoon of the first day, as cooking smells of the nightly meal that would break their fast began to waft through the house, she was ravenous. She persevered each day, however, determined not to give in. By the end of the week she was managing to make it through the day with little trouble. She could see that Zahra was impressed with her and she took pride in this, but when food was finally served after sundown she was famished. The hardest part of it all was watching Zahra and Aza eat. She served them and then waited for her turn, all the while trying desperately to keep her belly from rumbling too loudly.

At the end of Ramadan there was a feast. And what a feast! The women in the kitchen spent the whole day preparing food and cakes and sweets. After they had eaten, Zahra took Angeline by the hand and led her up to the roof of the house. Aza danced around them this time, wild with excitement. It was dark by then, and Angeline caught her breath as she saw all the streets and the mosques brightly lit up. Shooting streamers of fire and sparks of stars illuminated the sky, and she held her hands over her ears at the sounds of the explosions they made. Then she had to make a grab for Aza as the child nearly bounced off the roof in her enthusiasm.

Rugs had been spread for the women to lie on, and cushions. Behind them was a pigeon coop. Nearly every house in the city had a coop on its roof. Messages were sent from place to place by pigeons and the skies of Cairo were alive with the birds during the day. Now they rustled and made anxious little sounds, disturbed, no doubt, by all the unusual noise.

The women reclined there, watching the display until nearly dawn. The other concubines were there as well and their children played with Aza. The Emir's wives, heavily veiled, sat in a curtained pagoda at one end of the roof. Angeline tried to pick out Nusaybah, but she could not be certain which one she was. None of them made any sign of recognizing her.

For the next three days they celebrated Id al-Fitr, the festival that marked the end of Ramadan. Everyone received new clothes to wear. Angeline was given a shift of the softest, brightest red cotton and golden slippers. Finally she was allowed out with Samah to go and see the celebrations that were taking place all over the city. She saw magicians and puppet shows. Minstrels and musicians played and sang on every corner. There was even an old man with a basket full of snakes that coiled and uncoiled themselves around him as he sat cross-legged in the dirt. Angeline stared in horror when he picked one up and kissed it on the nose.

Tucked away at the end of one street, a storyteller held the crowds enthralled. Angeline tugged Samah toward him and would not budge until they had listened to his story about a foolish weaver who lost all his wares and who was only saved by the son he had banished in anger. By now she could understand almost every word. To her surprise, far from objecting, stolid, rigid Samah was as spellbound by his tale as she.

It was a magical day. Angeline recounted every instant of it to Father Martin and Stephen when she saw them next. Father Martin was silent and disapproving as usual, but Stephen asked question after question, interested in spite of himself. Angeline was certain she saw a look of longing in his eyes.

Stephen is more of a slave than I am, she thought as she left to return to Zahra, her high spirits dampened. She could not help feeling annoyed. It is by his own doing, she fumed. He will not allow himself to go out and see what there is to see here. How can anybody possibly help him?

"We are going on an excursion, my little Angeline," Zahra said on the evening of the last day of Id al-Fitr. "In two days' time our Master is going to take us on an expedition where you will behold wonders greater than you have ever imagined."

She would say no more, no matter how much Angeline pressed, so for the next two days Angeline lived in suspense. The whole house was in a fever of preparation. The Emir was taking two of his wives, Samah told her. The eldest refused to go because she thought the trip would be too arduous, but Nusaybah would be one of the other two.

"Where *are* we going?" Angeline demanded, but Samah, under Zahra's strict orders, would not tell her, even though the woman had been much friendlier since their day out together during Id al-Fitr. She hadn't yanked Angeline by the arm or pinched her for weeks.

Of the concubines, only Zahra was chosen,

and Angeline was to accompany her. The jealousy in the harem when this was announced was so thick in the air that it could have been spread like honey. Yet another grievance for Anka, Heba, and the other two slave girls to hold against her, Angeline thought, but she was too caught up in the excitement to care. Aza sulked because, again, she was to stay with Samah.

"No children are permitted to accompany us," Zahra said.

"Habib is going," Aza answered rebelliously.

Zahra frowned at her.

"He is the son of the Emir," she said reprovingly. "A prince can go where a slave's child cannot."

Aza stuck out her lower lip and flounced over to a corner of the room. For the rest of the morning she refused to play or even talk to anyone.

Angeline could not help but feel sorry for her. She was pleased when Stephen said that he was to go, however. Finally! Finally he would get out and start living again! To her surprise, Father Martin did not disapprove.

"I would go myself," he said. "I have heard of these wonders in the desert. But I am too ill. I could not make the journey."

At that, Angeline looked at him more closely. His face was drawn and white. She felt a pang of guilt as she realized that she had not noticed it before. She saw Stephen looking at him, his eyes worried.

"Should I stay with you?" he asked.

Angeline held her breath, then let it out with a sigh of relief when Father Martin replied.

"No, my son," he said. "This is something you must see."

"What is it?" Angeline demanded. "Zahra will not tell me."

"Some edifices the ancient Egyptians built. So long ago that no one rightly remembers when. Magnificent structures," Father Martin replied. "I have heard of them, but cannot begin to imagine what they must look like. I know only that they are a wonder and must be seen."

"Buildings?" Angeline persisted.

"Buildings, but not buildings," Father Martin replied. "You must see them," he repeated. "And when you return, you must tell me of them."

They left at dawn, just after the morning prayers. Their entourage was made up of an enormous number of people and beasts that wound its way through the wakening streets of Cairo. A party of the Emir's own Mamluks, his private army of slave soldiers, rode tough, wiry war horses and went first to clear the way. Abd'al Haseeb followed on the most magnificent Arabian stallion that Angeline had ever seen. The colour of honey, it had a pale, flowing mane and tail and pranced through the congested streets like a prince amongst beasts. Habib followed him on a frisky pony, sitting tall and proud in his saddle, looking neither to the right nor the left. Small though he was, in his long golden robe and crimson turban, he looked every bit a prince. He even wore a sabre at his waist.

Behind them came slaves and servants, some on donkeys, others on camels. To Angeline's astonishment, Stephen rode past her on a camel. He did not see her and looked more than a little anxious. Angeline suspected that he was holding on for dear life. In front of him rode Zeid on a mule. As they passed, Angeline saw Zeid turn and call out something to Stephen. Words of encouragement, perhaps, but the general noise and shouting was such that she could not hear him.

The Emir's wives came next in two litters. Behind Angeline and Zahra walked a multitude of slaves carrying tents and provisions. Zahra was still being mysterious about the whole venture, but she did tell Angeline that they would be staying overnight, returning the next day.

They made their way to the river. Small boats waited for them there, much like the one that had brought Angeline, Stephen, and Father Martin to Cairo. Angeline stopped and stared at them, remembering the day she had first stepped ashore here, so long ago, it now seemed. How her life had changed since then! Zahra gave her a little push, and startled out of her memories, she made haste to take hold of the boatmen's hands and stepped into their boat.

On the other side of the river, the whole procession reassembled itself to resume its journey, but this time the women were to ride in litters fastened atop camels—sturdily Angeline hoped as she looked at them dubiously. The camels lay on the ground, their legs tucked under them. Zahra was handed in, then reached out to help Angeline. Angeline allowed herself to be lifted up. When they were settled, the camel stood up. She screamed. It was truly frightening. The beast straightened up its back legs first and the whole litter lurched forward. Then, with a great heaving, the camel straightened its front legs and they swayed up with it. Angeline could not help herself—she clutched onto the sides of the litter in terror. Zahra, sitting relaxed beside her, laughed. Then the camel started to move with a rocking, rolling gait.

At first Angeline sat hunched up and hung on with all her strength, certain that they would fall, but after a while, she summoned up the courage to look out through the curtains at the passing view.

The passing view was mostly sand.

The sun rose and she began to feel quite warm, but Zahra insisted that it was still cool and kept her shawl tucked around her.

I do not think Zahra would have liked snow very much, Angeline thought.

They travelled for the best part of the morning, then stopped for the midday prayer. The camel driver tapped the beast on its knees and it knelt. The litter lurched forward as it had done before, then the animal lowered its back legs. Once again Angeline's heart was in her throat until the camel finally settled on the ground.

It was good to walk and get the stiffness out of her legs, but they were deep in the desert here. There was no green anywhere, just shades of brown and yellow and rolling dunes stretching as far as she could see. The sun beat down and a slight breeze sifted sand into her face, down the neck of her shift, and into every fold of her skirt. She drew her scarf more tightly around her head, but she could feel sand in her hair as well. The ground beneath her feet burned through her light slippers. A slave brought a bladder of water. Zahra drank and then handed it to Angeline. Angeline tilted it up gratefully and gulped the water down. Her throat was dry—it felt as if *it* were coated in sand. Sand even gritted between her teeth.

And then, in the distance, through the haze of

the noon heat, she saw a strange, sharply pointed shape shimmering in the sunlight, towering toward the sky. She turned to Zahra.

"What is that?" she asked. "Is that where we are going?"

But Zahra would not answer. "Wait and you will see," was all that she would say.

Chapter Eleven

After the noon prayers, they ate some fruit and cheese, drank more water, then climbed back into the litter and started off again. The land rose sharply. Angeline rode peering out of the curtains, her eyes fixed on the strange shape in the distance. Soon she could detect two other similar but smaller shapes. Nothing could have prepared her for what she beheld when they reached the site, however: a huge three-sided edifice built of stones so big some were as tall as a man. She could barely contain her impatience while Zahra was helped out, then she leaped to the ground. She looked up at the pyramid towering above her and could not breathe for the awe of it. It seemed to pierce the sky itself. Never had she seen anything so immense! She felt drawn up into it—dizzy with the height of it. She had to tear her eyes away in order to regain her balance.

Two other triangular buildings sat behind the first, each slightly smaller than the previous one but, even so, they were enormous. The middle one had a rough cap of stone over the peak of it.

How could men have possibly built such structures?

She felt an irresistible urge to run over to the pyramid. To look at it more closely, to touch the stones and imagine what the weight of each one might be, but Zahra called to her.

"Stay here with me while the servants erect our tent," she ordered.

There was no disobeying Zahra of course, no matter how reluctant Angeline was, but it seemed that Habib was labouring under no such restrictions. He dismounted his pony and ran to the base of the great pyramid. He looked up, then unfastened the sabre at his waist, let it drop into the sand, and began to climb. Within seconds he had scrambled up the uneven stones, out of reach of the slaves who accompanied him. The slaves began to scramble after him, but they could not climb nearly as quickly as he could. He soon outstripped them.

Shouts and calls rang out, but the little prince paid them no heed. As Angeline watched, he climbed higher and higher. Though Angeline found herself admiring his nimbleness, she realized how foolhardy the child was. Surely he would have enough sense not to climb too high—but it seemed he did not.

Then it happened. He slipped and fell. Down onto the stones beneath him, then farther down onto a narrow ledge. Angeline heard a scream—she was certain it was Nusaybah. There was a moment of deathly silence as they all stared at the small, still figure lying motionless so far above them.

Someone broke away from the crowd and began to climb up to Habib. It was Stephen. Higher and higher he went, passing the slaves who were labouring so uselessly. Finally, he reached Habib and knelt beside the prince. Habib lifted his head and there was a collective sigh of relief from all those watching.

It was not to be so easy, though. Habib tried to stand, then crumpled back onto the narrow ledge. There was another gasp from the watching crowd. Another scream.

Stephen put an arm around Habib, under his shoulders, and helped him back to his feet.

Then, carefully, they began the descent. Angeline held her breath until they were finally on the ground. The little prince was immediately surrounded by people. The Emir himself strode over to them. Abd'al Haseeb bent down, picked Habib up, and carried him back to where his tent had already been erected. He disappeared inside.

Stephen was left standing at the base of the pyramid, staring after them. Zeid went up to him, touched him on the elbow, and led him away. Only then did Angeline see Nusaybah with her hands to her mouth, her shoulders bowed and shaking.

Zahra sent Angeline to fetch her evening meal from the cook tent; lamb that had been roasted over a pit and bowls of rice, beans, and vegetables. The scent of spices perfumed the air. While she was there she saw one of Nusaybah's servants make her way over to Zahra's tent. With news of the little prince, perhaps?

"Was Habib hurt badly?" Angeline asked once Zahra had finished. She took her own portion then, sat herself down on cushions piled up on one side of the tent, and began to eat, grease dripping down her fingers. She licked them one by one, savouring the richness.

"No," Zahra answered. "But his pride was." The tone of her voice left no doubt as to what she thought of the prince's impetuous behaviour. "Your friend, Stephen, was very brave. The Emir has told me about the journey that led you here," she added. "Your priest told Zeid the story. A foolish endeavour it seems to me, yet your friend was very courageous to take on such a challenge."

"Yes," Angeline answered. "He was."

She finished her meal in silence, grateful that Zahra said no more. She did not want to speak to Zahra of their crusade. How could she?

The sun was setting behind the pyramids now, casting an air of mystery over them and over the plateau on which they had camped. Someone in one of the other tents was plucking the strings of an 'oud. Its deep tones seemed to hover and dance around the ancient stones. Then a woman took up the melody and her voice wove more magic into the air.

"Who built these wondrous buildings?" Angeline asked.

"People who lived here in ancient times, so the Emir has told me," Zahra replied.

"How?" Angeline asked. "How could they have possibly raised such huge stones? How could they have formed them into such perfect shapes? And for what purpose?"

"No one knows," was all that Zahra could say.

Zahra stayed in the Emir's tent that night, but Angeline was not called to attend her. She lay alone in Zahra's tent. She had not seen Stephen since his rescue of Habib. I wonder how he is feeling, she thought. I wonder if Habib is grateful? Probably not, she thought with a wry smile. That prideful young boy is probably furious at having to be rescued. I hope the Emir is grateful. I'm sure Nusaybah is.

The next morning, after prayers and after they had broken their fast, they made ready to return to Cairo, but when Angeline and Zahra took their places in the litter, to Angeline's surprise they did not turn back the way they had come.

Zahra smiled. "There is still one more marvel to behold," she said.

As they made their way down from the height on which the pyramids stood, Angeline could make out another enormous stone shape. Not a pyramid; as they drew closer she could see it was a gigantic head set on massive shoulders that disappeared down into the sand beneath them. There was a hint of a colossal body crouching out behind it. The head was that of a man wearing a curious kind of headdress. His face was pitted and scarred by the ravages of time.

"What is that?" Angeline asked again. "Did the same people make this? Whose face is it?"

"Another mystery," Zahra said. "Our land is full of mysteries. But they say the face is the image of one of the ancient rulers of this land—Pharaohs, they were called. And there are old stories that say this is but the head of some unimaginably great animal whose body has been covered with sand over the years since it was carved. A lion, perhaps, such as you have seen in pictures in the Emir's books."

There was a stillness to the face that mesmerized Angeline. She allowed the camel driver to help her down from the litter and stood in the sand to stare up at it, entranced, unaware of the others who chattered and milled around her. When Zahra called to her to come back, it was as if she had been awakened from a dream.

She spoke little on the return to Cairo. Her mind was too full of what she had seen. A land full of mysteries, indeed. But such a land. And such a people those ancient ones must have been. No wonder Ibrahim was so proud of being descended from them. A strange feeling was growing inside her. At first she could not recognize it but then, as the rolling motion of the camel's gait rocked and soothed her, as she stared out at the endless dunes of sand, she realized what it was.

She felt at peace.

When next Angeline saw Stephen there was a difference in him. He rose when she entered the classroom and greeted her with a smile and eyes that were brighter than she had seen in a long time.

"I am released from my duties with that evil old tyrant, Kareem," he said. "The Emir was so grateful for my saving his son that he has liberated me from that hateful job. Mind you, I am now to be nursemaid to the boy!"

"Not nursemaid," Father Martin put in. "You are to be his guardian. It is a great honour, Stephen."

"Yes, I suppose so," Stephen replied. His mouth twisted and his eyes dimmed for a moment. "A great honour for a *slave.*"

But not so great an honour for one who was to lead thousands to the liberation of Jerusalem, Angeline thought, and knew that Stephen was thinking the same. He said no more, and Father Martin summoned them to work.

When they had finished and Father Martin left, Stephen reached out to Angeline and caught her by the arm.

"Will you stay a moment?" he asked.

As soon as Father Martin was out of earshot he spoke again.

"Do you still see that boy? That Coptic boy?"

"I do," Angeline replied. "Quite often." She had been back several times since she had told Ibrahim the tale of their journey and they had talked much. She had come to think of him as a good friend. She was still anxious to arrange a meeting between him and Stephen, but had not been able to figure out how it might be done. She so rarely had the opportunity of speaking alone with Stephen; Father Martin was nearly always with them and she did not want to speak of the Coptic boy in front of him. The priest was often out of sorts these days and she feared his disapproval.

"I have some mornings to myself now," Stephen said, "when the Emir takes Habib hunting with their falcons. If I met you in the suq, would you take me there?"

"I most certainly would!" Angeline exclaimed. "When will you next be free?"

"I will let you know," Stephen replied.

At last, Angeline thought. At last Stephen was taking an interest in *something!*

It was not long until the opportunity presented itself.

"Tomorrow," Stephen whispered to her one afternoon as they finished up their lessons and prayers with Father Martin. His eyes were gleaming.

By great good fortune, Zahra had no errands for Angeline the next day, so after leaving Aza with her teacher, Angeline made her way to the suq. She saw Stephen waiting for her and ran to him. Then she forced herself to slow down and walk discreetly. It would not do to draw attention to themselves.

"I hope Ibrahim will be there," she said, but even as she spoke the words she saw the boy coming out of the church.

Ibrahim brightened as he saw her.

"Welcome," he called out as they approached him. "Have you been well?"

"I have," Angeline called back. "And I have finally brought my friend to meet you."

The two boys looked at each other a little warily, then Ibrahim smiled. "Angeline has told me about you," he said.

At that, Stephen's face clouded.

"Has Angeline told you of our journey and why we undertook it?" Stephen asked.

"Yes," Ibrahim answered. "I wish that you would tell me more."

"Perhaps . . . In time . . ." Stephen answered.

Ibrahim seemed to sense his reluctance. He quickly changed the subject.

"Will you come into the church?" he asked. "Our priest is there—I'm certain that he would like to meet you."

"No," Stephen replied, too hastily. "I thank you, but I would rather talk here."

They found a patch of shade and sat, chatting, while the sun rose higher in the sky. Angeline marvelled at the ease with which Stephen spoke. He had learned far more Arabic than she, and often interpreted something for her that she had not understood. Truly, Stephen must have a gift for learning languages, she thought.

Stephen avoided any mention of their journey. Instead, he asked Ibrahim about his life. "My father works at the Citadel with the Sultan al-Adil himself, Ibrahim said with pride. "I will work with him next year when I have learning enough." At that he glanced skywards and added quickly, "And I must be going to my school now. I have overstayed my allotted time here." He rose to his feet. Angeline and Stephen got to theirs as well.

"Will you return?" Ibrahim asked Stephen.

Stephen hesitated, then answered. "Yes," he said. "Yes, I will."

"Good," said Ibrahim. "It will be interesting

to have another Franj for a friend. Quite unusual."

Angeline leaped in at that. It reminded her of something Ibrahim had said at their first meeting and that she had forgotten.

"You said that the Copts do not like the Franks," she said. "Why is that?"

"We Copts have been much oppressed," Ibrahim replied, his face suddenly serious. "But as I said, we are the true Egyptians, descendants of the Pharaohs. St. Mark himself brought Christianity to us in the thirty-fifth year after the death of our Lord Jesus. The Romans ruled us then, and they persecuted us until they, too, converted to the true faith. Now you Franj and your Pope do not wish to recognize us. You say we are not true Christians, that we are heretics. The Arabs who came with the religion of Islam are the only ones who have not persecuted us."

"But we believe in the same God," Angeline said.

"We do," Ibrahim agreed.

Stephen stared at Ibrahim, brow furrowed, but he said nothing.

Chapter Twelve

"Aza is a lovely child," Angeline said one day as she was amusing her, as usual, by drawing pictures. No more ugly pictures of Heba and Anka and the other two, though. "What will become of her?" She asked the question carelessly, not really thinking about what she was saying. "Will she be a concubine, too?"

"Never!"

She looked up at Zahra, startled by the fierceness of her reply.

"She is not a slave," Zahra said. "Children of slaves are born free—the Emir will provide for her for life because she is his daughter, but she will be a free woman. And one day I will be free, too, and we will leave here."

"But I thought you were happy here." Angeline was confused. "And how will you be free? How will that happen?"

"This work that I do—the copying of books for the Emir's library—I am working to buy my freedom."

"You can *buy* your freedom?"

"I can. Any slave can with the Emir's permission. It is considered to be an act of devotion for a Muslim to free a slave."

Angeline fell silent, but her mind was on fire. A slave could buy her freedom! That meant that she could, too. She did not even stop to think about what she would do with freedom if she achieved it—it would be enough not to be a slave, not to be a servant to anyone.

She looked at Zahra. She was bent over her work once again, concentrating hard. *That* would be Angeline's way out, too. She was good at the copying—Zahra had told her so. She would learn more, become even better—as good as Zahra.

"Would you let me do a page of your work?" she asked. "Could I help you?"

Zahra raised an eyebrow. "What are you thinking, binty? I can see your mind whirling."

"If I worked hard," Angeline said. "If I could learn to do the work as well as you, could I work to earn my freedom, too?"

Zahra stared at Angeline thoughtfully, as if something had just occurred to her.

"It is possible," she answered. "The Emir will have need of a copyist when I go—and Allah willing, that will not be too long from now. Here," she said, holding out the book from which she had been copying. "Here in this book is a page that is very short. Let me see what you can do with it."

Angeline took the page to be copied and a sheet of fresh, clean paper with trembling hands and immediately almost spilled the ink all over it. Zahra's eyebrow rose again, but she said nothing.

Angeline worked for the rest of the day on that page. She understood nothing of what she was copying, of course, but that was of no matter. Just before Salat al-Maghrib, the call to evening prayer, sounded out, she showed it to Zahra.

"Almost good enough," she said.

"Almost!" Angeline exclaimed. She looked at her work. She had been so proud of it.

"Yes, almost," Zahra repeated. "Here, let me show you what needs improvement." She beckoned Angeline to sit beside her. Angeline blushed with shame as Zahra pointed out small errors and ungraceful strokes.

"I thought you believed my work to be good!" she finally burst out. "You were proud of it. You showed it to the others."

"And it is good," Zahra said. "Very good, otherwise I would not for one moment encourage you to think you might one day take my place. But it is not good enough for the Emir. He demands perfection."

Then perfection he shall have, Angeline thought grimly, and set herself to copying the page yet again.

"Zahra is teaching me to be a copyist," Angeline proclaimed proudly when next she saw Stephen and Father Martin. "Did you know that she is working to buy her freedom that way? And if I become good enough, I could do so as well. I could buy *my* freedom!"

She was expecting enthusiasm but did not receive it.

"Do you really think that could happen?" Father Martin asked. The tone of his voice left no doubt that he was skeptical, and Stephen turned quickly away, but not before Angeline had seen the look on his face.

Angeline bit her lip. How could she not have realized what Stephen would feel? And then yet another thought struck her. What would she do if she were freed and Stephen were still a slave? What would happen then?

"Perhaps you could buy your freedom as well . . . ?" she began, but the words sounded hollow even to her ears.

Stephen flushed. "Doing what?" he demanded. "Nurse-maiding a child?"

"But you can read and write now," Angeline said. "And you speak Arabic well. I have heard you. Perhaps . . . ?" Her voice trailed off.

Stephen shrugged. "I am pleased for you," he said. "You need not worry about me." He would say no more.

Angeline fell silent. Did she really want her freedom if Stephen had to remain bound in slavery? What would happen to the two of them then? She looked at him as he sat across from her, absorbed in his work. She could not give up the dream to escape her slavery, but neither could she imagine life without Stephen.

And her cheeks still burned at the memory of his touch.

Zahra had another table set up beside hers. She procured good quills and paper for Angeline. She sent Aza off with Samah in the afternoons so that Angeline would have time to work. But, now that Angeline was serious about submitting work to Abd'al Haseeb, Zahra was much more critical. Days passed when she did not praise Angeline at all, only found fault. At those times Angeline despaired.

"If it is too difficult for you, you may give it up," Zahra said one afternoon when Angeline had thrown her quill down in disgust, spattering a piece of paper with ink and ruining it completely.

"Never!" Angeline snapped back and gritted her teeth. She would show her.

"Then kindly do not spoil good paper with your temper," Zahra said.

Angeline took a deep breath and picked the quill up again. She pulled the spoiled piece of paper toward her and copied out the phrase that had defeated her. Then she copied it again. And yet again. Finally, she showed it to Zahra.

"That will do," Zahra said. Her face was blank, but she handed Angeline a fresh paper. "Do this page as skilfully," she said, "and I might include it with my work for the Emir to see."

Angeline felt tears rising. She turned her head away, embarrassed, and scrubbed the back of her hand across her eyes, then set to work again. This work would be judged by the Emir himself!

She became so immersed that when the call to Salat al-Maghrib came she looked up, shocked that so much time had passed. She tidied her materials and handed the sheets of paper she had been working on to Zahra, then held her breath.

"Very good," Zahra said. She looked up from the papers to Angeline, and finally smiled. "*Very* good, binty. The Emir will be pleased." She rose, stretched, and beckoned Angeline to help her make ready to wash and pray.

That night, just as she was about to fall asleep, Angeline realized something with a jolt. She had snapped at Zahra. Slaves did not snap at their mistresses. But Zahra had not rebuked her for it, only for spoiling the paper. She thought back over the day—over the past several days. Gradually, her relationship with Zahra had changed and she had not even noticed. She still ran errands for Zahra, still waited on her and helped her to dress, still slept on cushions outside the Emir's room when Zahra went to him, but Zahra did not treat her as a slave anymore. She treated her more as a student. Almost as an equal. But she *was* still a slave, Angeline reflected bitterly. Nothing had changed that.

The weather was hot again, the brief winter over. A dry wind that Zahra told Angeline was called the "khamsin" blew steadily every day and brought in the dust from the desert. Angeline felt as if it were scratching and searing every nerve in her body. Even Zahra was often ill-tempered and out of sorts. The four slave girls—the four devils, as Angeline called them in her mind—seemed to be inspired in new ways to make her life a torment. She tried to avoid them, but it was impossible.

Stephen, too, was moody. Angeline could not help feeling that she was a good part of the cause of it now—that Stephen brooded because of her work with Zahra, her plans for gaining her freedom. She could not help feeling guilty, but that made her angry as well. She had asked him several times to go back with her to the Coptic Christian church, but he would not. As the days passed, Angeline worried more about Father Martin as well. He was so gaunt that his face looked almost like a skeleton. Never did he complain, but she often saw him wince as he rose from his desk.

"He is ill, Stephen," she said one day after he had left them.

"I know," Stephen agreed. "But he will do nothing about it. The Emir has skilled men of medicine, but he will not let them come near him."

She had not seen Nusaybah again. Nor did Habib dally after his lessons anymore.

"Habib spends more time with his father now," Stephen said. "And he sees his mother more often as well." He smiled. "When he fell, the first person he cried for was his mother."

Angeline was pleased to hear this, but she missed Nusaybah. The woman had intrigued her.

The khamsin subsided, then the heat set in. Heat such as Angeline had never known. No amount of juice or water could assuage her thirst, no amount of fanning could cool her. Zahra, however, who had brooded in the coolness of the winter, seemed to thrive in the summer. She worked tirelessly. Angeline could not believe that Zahra did not sweat! Drops of perspiration ran down her own face without ceasing. She had to wipe them away constantly, always fearful that she would drip onto her precious paper and mar it. Her quill was slippery in her fingers and more than once caused her to make mistakes in the intricate characters she copied. She tied her hair back but it hung heavy and darkly wet on her neck. Her daily bath in the hamman was her only respite, but even then the water was so warm that it was barely refreshing. The river water that was brought up by camels every morning was hardly cooler. Angeline found herself longing for snow. She forgot how her hands and feet had frozen, how it had felt to huddle shivering in a threadbare blanket. She could only remember the freshness of it. The coldness of it on her tongue. She found herself dreaming of the icy cold water of the mountain streams through which they had passed on their crusade, even as she tossed and turned on sweat-soaked pillows at night.

Now the Coptic church became a refuge for her. There, in the cool dimness, she could snatch a few moments of relief from the relentless, burning sun. One especially hot day, she and Stephen waited in the schoolroom in vain for Father Martin. Then a servant came with word that he was too ill to teach that day, nor would he teach the next.

"I have permission to go see Ibrahim tomorrow," Angeline told Stephen. "It is a Friday, the Muslim holy day, and Zahra sometimes gives me leave to go then. She spends most of the day in prayer and Samah takes care of Aza. If you are not going to work with Father Martin, then come with me. Ibrahim has asked many times about you. Habib will be at the mosque with his father, Father Martin is ill—what else is there for you to do? It is cool there." And comforting, she added silently.

Stephen looked as if he would decline as he usually did, but this time Angeline was having none of it.

"I will bother you and tease you until you agree," she said. Her words were light, but there was iron behind them.

Stephen heard it. He surrendered.

"Very well," he said. "I will go with you."

Elated, Angeline set off with him the next morning. It was early yet—they had the whole day ahead of them. A perfect gift. They made their way down the winding, dusty alley. Even this early in the day the heat was intense. There was not a cloud in the hard blue sky, not a breath of a breeze. The leaves on the trees hung limp and motionless. By the time they reached the church, Angeline was panting. She and Stephen had not spoken much—it was too hot to talk. Her shift clung to her body; Stephen's tunic was dark with sweat. They walked through the arched doorway into the still darkness with relief.

Angeline sank down onto a pew and bowed her head. She would not listen to Mass in this church, but she would pray. God would listen to her here as well as anywhere else, she was certain of it. Stephen sat beside her, his head bowed, but she knew he was not praying.

There was no one else inside. Angeline was

disappointed not to see Ibrahim, then she felt a hand on her shoulder.

"Welcome," a voice whispered.

She looked up into Ibrahim's dark eyes. As usual, he smiled. He turned to Stephen.

"It is good to see you here again, Franj. I have missed you. How have you been keeping?"

Stephen started. He had been deep in reverie and had not noticed Ibrahim standing there.

"Well . . ." he stuttered. "I am well."

"Do you have time today for talk?" Ibrahim asked.

"We do," Angeline answered before Stephen could say anything. "We have the whole day."

Ibrahim's smile grew wider.

"Then I have a suggestion," he said. "Come home with me. I would like you to meet my family."

"We could not do such a thing," Stephen replied stiffly. "It would not be seemly. We would be imposing on your privacy."

"Oh, Stephen," Angeline hissed. "Be not so righteous. We would love to accompany you," she said to Ibrahim. She was alive with curiosity to see how Ibrahim lived here in Cairo. To find out more about these Coptic Christians.

"You would not be intruding at all," Ibrahim said. "In truth," he added, his smile turning now into a sly grin, "my family is most intrigued by my stories of you, Franj. They greatly desire to meet you."

Angeline leaped to her feet.

"Then let us go," she said. "Who knows? There might not be another opportunity."

Ibrahim turned to lead the way out; Angeline made haste to follow him. She looked back at Stephen, who was hesitating.

"Come, Stephen," she hissed with a shake of her head. *"Come!"*

He frowned. For a moment Angeline thought he would refuse, then he gave in.

Ibrahim led them out of the church. He turned down a narrow street that took them in a direction Angeline had not yet explored.

"My house is not far," Ibrahim said. "My mother will be so pleased to see you," he added to Angeline. "She is curious about you. About how a Christian girl manages in a Muslim household."

She had not thought of this—that she would be questioned by Ibrahim's mother! What if the woman disapproved of her? What if she disapproved of Ibrahim's friendship with a slave so much that she forbade him to see her again?

"And my father might be there, as well," Ibrahim went on, deepening Angeline's foreboding.

Perhaps this was not a good idea after all. Angeline caught Stephen's eye.

"Perhaps this is not wise . . ." Stephen began, echoing her thoughts.

"Of course it is," Ibrahim hastened to reassure him. "I am always wise," he said with mock arrogance. Then he sobered. "Truly, my parents are good people. They will welcome you, you need not fear."

"They welcome slaves?" Stephen asked. He could not keep the gall from his voice.

"They will not think of you as slaves," Ibrahim replied. "We do not keep any. It is not our way. They will welcome you as fellow Christians." Then he spoiled the reassurance somewhat by adding, "Even if you are Franj."

Angeline's misgivings only increased, however, when she saw the house into which Ibrahim was leading them. Almost as imposing as the Emir's, it was a tall, many-storeyed stone building, surrounded by a high mud brick wall. As soon as they passed through the gate, they were encircled by a lush, fragrant, flower-filled garden. Doors opened off the garden on three sides. Ibrahim led the way to one of them. A servant appeared and bowed low.

"Nicula, will you tell my mother that I bring friends?" Ibrahim ordered.

The servant scurried off. Angeline saw two others hurry to meet him and hear his message.

Slaves they may not keep, Angeline thought,

now thoroughly dismayed, but servants they certainly have aplenty. She was beginning to think that coming here was a mistake, indeed. There was naught to do but follow Ibrahim as he showed them into the house, however.

Ibrahim took them into a large, airy room that opened onto the courtyard. Tapestries hung on the walls, rich carpets covered flagstone floors, but a full-sized table stood in the middle, surrounded by benches. A woman rose from a couch to greet them. She was dressed in a light, filmy cotton gown. Her jet-black hair was drawn back and fastened with a golden clip. It tumbled down past her shoulders, nearly to her waist. The woman was almost the same age as Angeline's mother had been. Darker of skin than her mother, but there was something in her smile that was so like Marithe's that it snatched Angeline's breath away.

Ibrahim spoke a few words to her in their own Coptic language, then introduced her to Stephen and Angeline.

"This is my mother, Mariam," he said. His voice held much affection.

Mariam reached to give him a quick hug, then held out a hand to Angeline.

"Welcome, my child," she said. "How good it is to meet you. Ibrahim has spoken so much of you."

Angeline took her hand. It felt so like her own mother's that for one mad moment she felt like throwing herself into this woman's arms and pressing her head to her breast as she had done so often with Marithe. Her throat constricted; she could make no answer.

Ibrahim's mother gave her hand a squeeze, then turned to Stephen.

"And you are welcome here as well, Stephen," she said. "We have heard somewhat of your troubles. Perhaps you will find some peace here."

Caught unawares, Stephen's face softened. For one moment Angeline even thought she saw a glint of tears, then he lifted his chin and shook back the lock of hair that always fell in his eyes. Angeline was stunned. It was the same gesture he had used to make before beginning to preach.

"I thank you," he said.

"You will join us for our noon meal? Ibrahim's father will not be here, but I fear his brothers and sisters will. You will bear with them, I hope. They are most noisy and undisciplined." Her smile belied the criticism.

Angeline heaved a sigh of relief. She felt comfortable with Mariam; she would much rather not meet Ibrahim's father. Not yet, anyway.

No sooner had Mariam finished speaking than what seemed like a horde of laughing, boisterous children spilled into the room. There were only four, two girls and two boys, but true to their mother's warning, they made enough noise for an army. They surrounded Angeline and Stephen, bursting with questions.

"Enough!" Mariam commanded. "Seat yourselves and remember your manners!"

She showed Angeline and Stephen to chairs at one end of the table on either side of her. The children calmed and took their places as well. Mariam spoke a few words of blessing, then the servants brought in bowls of rice and beans, platters of smoking lamb and chicken, bread, cheese, and baskets of fruit. There were goblets of hibiscus juice as well.

Stephen spooned rice onto his plate while fending off questions from the boy—a smaller version of Ibrahim—who sat beside him and rattled queries off without pause for breath. Stephen seemed amused by the child.

Angeline watched him, then added a silent prayer of her own before she reached for the nearest bowl.

Thank you, dear Lord, for leading us to this house. For giving us Ibrahim as a friend.

Chapter Thirteen

For the rest of the summer, Angeline and Stephen visited Ibrahim's house whenever they could—mostly on Fridays, whenever Zahra gave Angeline leave and Father Martin could be persuaded to let Stephen off. They met Ibrahim's father, Yousef. To Angeline's relief he was as kindly as Mariam. He seemed to take pleasure in talking with them, especially with Stephen.

"Yousef says our priests have the wrong idea about the Coptic religion," Stephen told her one day as they walked back to the Emir's house. "He says that they worship our Lord as do we—

that they have been misunderstood. He would like to talk with Father Martin some time."

"Father Martin would never consent," Angeline said.

"I know. I would not even ask him," Stephen replied. "Still, it is a shame. Father Martin is lonely here."

Father Martin lonely? Angeline had not ever considered that. Indeed, she realized that she had not thought overly much about Father Martin at all. He was a priest—she had supposed that God was comfort enough for him.

On another day, some weeks later, Angeline stood watching Stephen and Ibrahim scuffling with Ibramin's two little brothers in their courtyard. The two boys had wrestled Stephen to the ground and were sitting on him, crowing with triumph. Stephen was groaning in mock surrender while Ibrahim tried to pull them off. The sight warmed her heart and brought a smile to her face. She looked up as Yousef came to stand beside her.

"Stephen begins to heal, I believe," he said.

Angeline could only nod. "That is what I pray for," she said.

"He tells me that you work with the concubine, Zahra, copying the great books from the Emir's library."

"Stephen told you that?" Angeline asked.

"Yes," Yousef answered. "He is very proud of you."

Angeline looked at him, startled.

"I am most interested," he went on, not seeming to notice her surprise. "I am fortunate enough to know Sultan al-Adil well, and I have had many opportunities to read the books in the palace library. It is a wondrous collection. There are many great works there. It must give you much pleasure to copy them. Tell me, can you read them as well?"

"At first I could not," Angeline answered. "But I am learning," she hastened to add.

"Good," he said, nodding his head. "It is worthy work that you do."

As they made their way home that day, Angeline kept darting curious looks at Stephen out of the corner of her eye. He was proud of her work! Could it be that he was not jealous of it after all? That he did not condemn her for it? She almost summoned up nerve enough to ask him, but not quite.

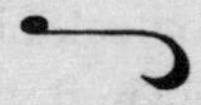

The summer wore on. Then Angeline realized that it was the month of September. The Muslims kept their own reckoning, but Father Martin insisted on keeping careful track of the days according to the Christian calendar. He celebrated all the Christian feast days and holidays, and would not let Angeline and Stephen forget them.

September!

They had been in Egypt for a year.

Neither Stephen nor Father Martin mentioned it, so she did not either, but Angeline could not help looking back and remembering. How terrified she had been on that day when Samah had dragged her away from Stephen and Father Martin and up to Zahra's room. How much had changed since then. She still knew not what the future held for her, but it no longer seemed as hopeless as it had then. She had something to look forward to now—her freedom.

September was an important month for Ibrahim as well.

"It is the beginning of the Coptic New Year," he announced that Friday when they met him at the church. "Thout, we call it. We used to celebrate Nawruz at this time. It was a very rowdy celebration and often got out of hand, so it has been forbidden now, but we still light bonfires and make merry around them. Will you come and join us?"

There was no possible way that Angeline would be allowed to visit Ibrahim's house during the evening, but Stephen was under no such restriction. When, to her surprise, he accepted the invitation, he was given permission to go. Even though she was pleased to see him do so, Angeline could not help a small, niggling feeling of resentment. After all, Ibrahim had been her friend first. She had come to feel at home in his family; she wanted to be part of their celebration, too. She did not dare to go so far as to complain to Zahra, but Zahra realized that she was sulking and soon wormed the reason out of her. Far from being annoyed, however, Zahra only laughed.

"Do not worry, binty," Zahra reassured her. "We have a great celebration of our own this month. It is the wafa an-Nil, *the Plenitude of the Nile*—the time when the Nile has reached its highest. This year it is especially full and the rejoicings will be great. I may have a special treat for you, you will see."

As was her wont, Zahra would say no more for the time being. She loved her secrets. Angeline hardly paid heed in any case, so envious was she of Stephen's liberty. She was even more envious when Stephen returned from Ibrahim's family celebration and described the bonfire and the feast that had followed it in great detail.

Then one morning Zahra came out of the Emir's rooms bursting with excitement.

"I have something to tell you," she said to

Angeline. "But after my bath. I will tell you when we are settled to work. It is great news."

Angeline was consumed with curiosity, but she knew well enough to hold her tongue as she followed Zahra to the hamman. Several other concubines were there. Zahra lolled in the water for an exceptionally long time. The others chattered away as usual, but Zahra lay silent, a small, secret smile on her lips. The other women noticed and cast glances at her out of the corners of their eyes, obviously as curious as was Angeline, but Zahra was enjoying her mystery. Only when they had returned to Zahra's room and settled down to work did she speak.

Angeline had taken up her quill, but Zahra stopped her.

"I have news for you, binty," she said. "Listen, now."

Angeline put the quill down.

"I took some pages of your work in to show the Emir last night. He was most impressed."

Angeline held her breath.

"He would like to see more."

Angeline reached for her quill eagerly. This *was* wonderful news indeed. But Zahra interrupted her yet again.

"That is not all, binty. Remember I told you that we celebrate the wafa an-Nil this month? Well, we are going to do so on the morrow. The

Nile has risen to sixteen cubits. Every year a dam is constructed to hold the waters back until they are certain that there is enough to irrigate the land. When this happens there is a great celebration and then the dam is broken and the waters are free to run to the sea. The Sultan himself will perform the takhliq al-miqyas. He crosses by boat to the Island of Rawda where the Nilometer is situated, and there he perfumes the waters as a ritual of good omen and gratitude. Only the most important of his Emirs are invited to escort him in their boats." She paused.

"Only the *most* important," she repeated. "Abd'al Haseeb will be one of them and *I* will accompany him!" She let out a peal of laughter. "The other concubines will writhe with envy. It took me most of the night to persuade him," she added. "It was difficult, but I can be very persuasive when I wish."

"That will be exciting for you," Angeline said. She was a little confused.

"But you do not know the rest of it," Zahra exclaimed. "When the Emir was so impressed with your work, I suggested that you come along, too. You could attend me and he could see you for himself."

"He agreed?" Angeline gasped. The words came out in a kind of squeak.

"He did," Zahra answered smugly.

"I am going on the Emir's boat?" Angeline squeaked again.

Zahra laughed. "You are, binty."

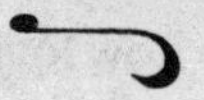

The next morning was a haze of confusion. Zahra bathed, and then bathed again. When Samah brought Aza to her she waved the child away with such curtness that Aza dissolved into a flood of tears. Angeline did her best to console her, but Zahra was so unreasonably anxious that Aza was given no time. Zahra tried on one gown after another. She rejected every one of them. She threw each in turn on the floor until the carpet was awash in brilliantly coloured silk. Finally, she determined upon one that shone with gold. She would be veiled, of course, but she darkened her eyes with kuhl and oiled her lashes.

Angeline had become expert at helping her, but when she had finished, to Angeline's surprise, Zahra turned to her.

"Your eyes, binty. Paint your eyes. And rouge your cheeks, too. You are Christian. You are allowed, and you will not need to be veiled. Let all see how pretty you are."

Angeline demurred, but there was no gainsaying Zahra.

Then, to her further astonishment, Zahra chose a deep blue gown from among the many on the floor and handed it to her.

"Wear this," she said. "It will suit your colouring. I want all to see how lovely my little slave is."

Angeline bridled at the word and made no move to accept the gown.

"Wear it, binty," Zahra said. It was a command.

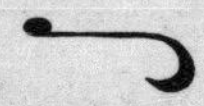

They set off in the early afternoon. Zahra led the way down through the house and out the gate in the back garden. Angeline slunk self-consciously behind her. She felt awkward and out of place in such fine clothes. Why had Zahra been so insistent? She had had to take the skirt up in the girdle at her waist, but it was still too long for her. Again, a litter borne by slaves awaited them. But there was no procession this time.

"The Emir has already gone ahead," Zahra explained.

Angeline made to open the curtains once the slaves had hoisted the litter up and set out at a brisk trot, but Zahra restrained her.

"I do not wish us to be looked upon," she said.

Angeline sank back, disappointed. The air

inside the heavily curtained litter quickly became hot and stuffy. Zahra took no notice of it, but it was becoming unbearable to Angeline.

"I am so hot," she said finally. "I am sweating. I will be a grievous mess by the time we reach the river."

Zahra frowned at her. She, of course, was showing no signs of the heat at all.

"Very well," she agreed, but reluctantly. "Part the curtains at your side just a little. Do not lean out!" she added sharply as Angeline yanked the drapes open and took a deep breath.

It was not a good notion. A barrage of noise and smells assaulted her. They were going through the street of the meat sellers—a man was slaughtering a lamb in front of a stall as they passed. The blood spurted out in a sudden gush and spattered the side of the litter. Angeline drew back quickly.

There was no breeze even with the curtains partly open, no lessening of the heat. A camel brushed past. It glared at Angeline out of the corner of one eye, then swished its tail so close to her nose that she put up a hand to ward it off.

"How can those beasts stink so?" she muttered.

Zahra merely raised an eyebrow.

"You were the one who wanted fresh air, binty. Not I."

Angeline drew the curtains shut again. She closed her eyes and tried to think of snow.

She felt the slaves set the litter down with a gentle bump. Angeline followed Zahra out, then stopped and stared, dumbfounded at the sight that greeted her. The river was crowded with boats, but not small boats such as the ones in which she had travelled before. These were large, brilliantly painted vessels flying scarlet, blue, and gold banners that whipped and snapped in the fitful breeze coming off the water. A multitude of richly dressed people thronged the bank.

Zahra gave her a sharp jab.

"Come along," she said.

The slaves pushed ahead of them, thrusting through the crowds and opening a path. Zahra walked tall and proud, looking neither to one side nor the other, but Angeline trotted behind her, head swivelling, trying at once to take everything in and not trip on her long skirt. They reached the riverbank. Awaiting them there was the Emir's boat, but this was not the boat in which Angeline and Stephen had been brought up to Cairo. It was far bigger. Eight men sat poised between four pairs of oars. Another white-clad boatman stood at the stern, rudder in hand. The deep crimson sails were furled. Scarlet and gold streamers flew from the mast. The boat itself gleamed deeply blue, so glossy that it reflected back glints of light from the water.

Zahra allowed herself to be guided up the plank that extended from the shore to the boat, and Angeline followed her gingerly. Hands reached for her and helped her down. They were escorted to the bow, where thick rugs had been spread and cushions piled in luxurious heaps. The Emir was seated there, dressed in the most formal of robes, one elbow draped over the railing. He was talking to another richly dressed man in an equally splendid boat that was tied up beside them. He smiled when he saw Zahra and beckoned her to come and sit beside him. She did so, then patted the cushions on her other side for Angeline. Angeline settled herself down, making a kind of nest for herself in the pillows and rugs, and waited to see what would happen.

Everyone, it seemed, was waiting. Servants brought juice and water. In the still heat of the afternoon, Angeline almost dozed. Zahra and the Emir conversed in low tones, but Angeline made no effort to hear what they were saying. There was enough breeze to keep the insects at bay, and the soft, gentle rocking of the boat was soothing. Then a murmur began from farther upriver and it travelled like a wave down to them.

A boat appeared. At first Angeline thought it

was a vision. It came into view shining with a brilliance that was almost unbearable to look at without shielding her eyes. As it drew nearer, she saw that the entire hull was plated with gold. The sun struck it and reflected off it in glinting rays. Angeline had thought the Emir's craft to be big, but this boat was more than ten times the size. It drew closer. Crimson sails billowed and caught the wind, but no less than sixty oars helped it speed on. A figure stood braced in the bow, clad in raiment that gleamed as brightly as the boat itself.

"Dhahabiyya," Zahra whispered. *The golden.* The boat of the Sultan himself.

The rowers took up their oars. All around them the others were doing the same. The boats of the Emirs sped to meet and usher the Sultan in. They all crossed to the bank of the Island of Rawda and there let down their anchors. The Emir rose to his feet and drew Zahra up beside him. Angeline, too, stood up and grasped the railing for support. She craned her neck to see what was happening.

The Sultan stepped off his boat onto the land. There a white-robed man awaited him, holding a cup. The Sultan dipped his hands into it.

"He is mixing saffron and musk," Zahra whispered. "To perfume and bless the waters."

"Who is that man who holds the cup?" Angeline asked.

"He is the guardian of the Nilometer," Zahra answered. "Watch now, see what he will do."

The Sultan stepped back. A slave was at his side immediately with a cloth with which to wipe his hands. The white-robed guardian held the cup for a moment, then he walked to the water's edge. Carefully holding the cup high, he walked into the water. Angeline held her breath as he went deeper and deeper. Finally, he was swimming.

"He will swim to the miqyas now," Zahra said.

Incredibly, the guardian did so, still holding the cup high with one hand. He reached the Nilometer, climbed the steps up to it, and poured the contents of the cup into it.

A long sigh escaped the onlookers.

As evening approached, the servants lit wax torches on the Emir's boat. All around them other torches were lit until the river was alive with dancing lights. The night brought a welcome coolness. Angeline had brought the soft woollen shawl that Zahra had given her and she was grateful for its warmth. The Emir's servants came with platters of sweetmeats and fruits, and spread them out on carpets for the Emir and Zahra. Zahra pulled Angeline toward her and handed her tidbit after tidbit.

"Is she not lovely?" she asked the Emir more than once.

Angeline was thankful for the darkness that hid her flaming cheeks. There was no need for the rouge that Zahra had made her wear and she scrubbed at it furtively whenever Zahra was not looking. She could not understand why Zahra persisted in drawing the Emir's attention to her. The Emir only laughed and never spoke to Angeline directly, but several times she caught him looking at her quizzically.

They crossed back to the Cairo riverbank, and stayed long into the night. On the shore musicians and singers performed. Men of learning recited from the Qur'an as well. When it was finally time to leave, Angeline stumbled down the plank after Zahra, half asleep. The Emir would remain to watch the breaking of the dam and pray in the nearby mosque, Zahra told her.

In the litter returning to the Emir's house Angeline did sleep. She barely woke enough to follow Zahra back to her room and help her make ready for bed.

"It turned out very well, I think," Zahra murmured as she blew out the wick and pulled a cover over her. "Just as I planned."

Angeline puzzled over the words as she tumbled onto her own couch, but sleep overcame her the moment she laid her head down. By morning she had forgotten them.

Chapter Fourteen

Now it was Angeline's turn to regale Stephen with her news.

"You sailed in the Emir's own boat?" Stephen asked when she had finished.

Pleased that he was so impressed, Angeline hastened to assure him that it was so.

"He did not speak to me, but he smiled," she said. Then she stopped. She caught her lip between her teeth and her brow furrowed.

"What is it?" Stephen asked. "What worries you?"

"Naught," Angeline responded quickly. But

there was an uneasiness in her mind that teased at her.

Stephen looked at her curiously, but did not press her further.

The weather cooled and winter was upon them once again. One morning Zahra gathered up the work that Angeline had done and smiled broadly.

"You are almost as good as I," she said. "The Emir agrees. He is most pleased with your copying."

Angeline felt her heart do a somersault within her chest.

"Is it good enough . . ." she began. "Do you think I could ask him if I could begin to work for my freedom?"

"I think you could," Zahra answered. "It will not be long now before I have earned my release. It would be good if you could take over from me then."

"But will you not stay here?" Angeline asked.

"No," Zahra answered. "Once I have my freedom I will leave."

"Where will you go?"

"I will take Aza, and we will find a place of our

own," Zahra said. She stood and walked to the window. A pigeon cooed on the sill. Absent-mindedly, she picked up a piece of bread that had been left over from her breakfast and began shredding it. She tossed the crumbs onto the sill and the pigeon pecked at them greedily.

"I have been planning this for so long," she said. Her voice took on a dreamlike quality. It sounded to Angeline almost as if she had forgotten that Angeline was there. As if she were speaking to herself.

"We will live by ourselves, Aza and I. I will set up as a copyist. Women make good livings for themselves that way. I will work for myself then, not for any master."

She caught herself, as if she had suddenly awoken from her reverie. She threw the rest of the crumbs out the window and turned back to Angeline.

"As for your question, binty," she said in her usual calm, brisk manner, "yes. I think you may speak to the Emir. I will arrange it."

Angeline worked even harder over the next few days, but her mind was not on the copying. She was mulling over Zahra's words. Perhaps this was something she could do as well when she had bought her own freedom.

But what of Stephen? The question that had

no answer. Did she really want her liberty so badly that she would leave him?

Angeline dared not mention the matter again, nor did Zahra speak of it. After a few days, she began to worry that Zahra had forgotten about it or had changed her mind. Then, one morning when Zahra came out of the Emir's rooms, she smiled at Angeline.

"You may speak to Abd'al Haseeb now, binty," she said.

"Now?" Angeline asked, aghast. "Go in to him now?"

"Yes," Zahra replied and gave her a push. "Imshi." *Off with you.* "He is waiting."

Angeline tried desperately to smooth her hair and straighten out her shift. Why had Zahra not given her more warning? She was still mussed and bemused by sleep.

"I look like an unkempt urchin!" she exclaimed.

"You look delightful," Zahra replied.

There was no arguing with her. Angeline pulled her fingers through her hair one last time, took a deep breath, and stepped through the doorway.

The Emir was reclining on pillows behind the low table when she entered. He was robed and dressed for the day. Angeline hesitated at the door. He beckoned to her.

"Come in," he said. He was smiling, his voice light and pleasant.

Angeline tried to calm the turmoil in her belly.

"So," the Emir said, "my Zahra tells me you wish to work to earn your freedom."

"I do," Angeline said. Her voice was thin and the words shook. "I do," she repeated more strongly.

"She has shown me your work. You have learned well," he said.

"Shukran, Maulaya," she replied. *Thank you, Master.* A year ago those words would have stuck in her throat.

"And how much do you think you are worth?" the Emir asked.

She looked at him in surprise. She had no idea how much he had paid for her. She had not thought of that.

"Not much?" she asked hopefully.

The Emir burst into laughter.

"Perhaps more than would be at first apparent," he said.

Angeline bit her lip and waited. She twisted her hands tightly together and willed her knees to stop shaking.

"Well, we shall see what you can do," the Emir said. He tilted his head to one side and looked at her more closely. "I shall miss my Zahra when she leaves me," he said.

Something in the tone of his voice sent an alarm jangling through Angeline. She was reminded of the way he had looked at her so appraisingly on the night of the Plenitude of the Nile, but he said no more, merely waved a hand at her in dismissal.

She backed out of the room, almost tripping over one cushion and treading awkwardly on another. In the hallway outside she fought to regain her composure.

The interview had unsettled her. She resolved not to mention it to Stephen when next she saw him, but when she entered the schoolroom, he was not there. Father Martin sat alone at the table. She paused for a moment, shocked at how wan his face was. He did not see her and, as she watched, passed a hand over his eyes and heaved a deep sigh.

"Are you not well, Father?" Angeline asked. She sat down beside him. She had thought often of the priest since Stephen's comment.

He straightened immediately.

"A small fever," he said. "It is nothing. It will pass."

She would have questioned him further but he forestalled her.

"Stephen will not be with us today. He has gone hunting with Habib and his father. But come, we will get on with your lessons."

Angeline set to work, but it was not the same without Stephen. After a short time she threw down her quill.

"I am feeling poorly too, Father," she said. "I think I will go now."

"Just as well," the priest replied. "You have made more mistakes today than you have in the past several weeks all put together. Go, then."

Zahra was working when Angeline returned to her room. Aza was playing at her feet. The child greeted her joyously.

"You are early today," Zahra said, looking up briefly.

"My head pains me," Angeline replied.

"I will send Samah for a remedy," Zahra said. She made as if to rise.

"No," Angeline said quickly. "It will pass."

"Play with me, then," Aza urged. "I am making a beautiful necklace for my mother." She grabbed a handful of beads from a basket and strew them on the floor before her.

Angeline sank down beside her. Absent-mindedly, she picked up some of the beads and began to string them on a cord. Zahra turned back to her work. Aza chattered without ceasing, but Angeline's mind was far away. She was remembering a girl she had befriended on the crusade. A girl who had chosen to stay in Marseilles and not join them on their ill-fated sea voyage. At the time she had felt sorry for Alys. Sorry that she would not be amongst the glorious few who had persevered and kept their faith. Who would be God's chosen to set the Holy City free.

Where was Alys now, she wondered. The woman who had offered Alys a home was a kind person. Alys probably had a good life there. Was she wed? Angeline wondered. Did she have a babe of her own? At that thought, sadness stabbed through her.

Her head did pain her. Madame Lafontaine would have had herbs to soothe it. She knew much about illnesses and remedies. She had offered to keep Angeline as well, but Angeline knew that the offer had been made only out of the goodness of her heart—she had no need of two girls. Angeline had refused.

Besides, she would never have left Stephen then.

The next week, when she returned to Father Martin, Stephen was there. She stopped short when she saw that his arm was bandaged.

"What happened?" she asked.

Stephen clutched the arm, but the look he gave her was one of pride.

"A jackal attacked me," he said. "I had to fight it off."

"How did you do so?" Angeline gasped. Her heart gave such a lurch that for a moment she could not breathe.

"In truth, I did not do much," Stephen admitted, but his eyes did not lose their glow. "I managed only to keep the beast away from Habib. It was Zeid who came to my aid. He slew the beast with his knife. But now the Emir has decreed that as Habib's guardian I may go armed as well." He dropped his hand to his belt and Angeline saw the dagger tucked into it.

Once her heart had settled back down, she could not help but delight in the sight of Stephen standing so tall and proud, but then her joy faded. The boy she had followed would have cast that knife aside, certain that his faith was all that he needed. Where was that faith now?

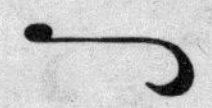

Angeline's head was aching again when she accompanied Zahra to the harem the next morning. The slave girls were dancing. The music snaked behind her eyes this day and set off wiry tendrils of pain.

When they had finished, Heba sidled up to Angeline.

"You are looking poorly," she said. She seemed pleased about it. She gave a flounce, setting the beads she had strung about her neck and waist to jingling. Her eyes were bright with satisfaction, her cheeks glowed from the exertion of the dance. She was beautiful—and looked as if she were well aware of it.

"I danced for the Emir again last night. He was enchanted with me. Zeid himself told me so." She turned to go, but cast a glance back over her shoulder.

"It is almost certain that he will choose me as a concubine. I will have power then." She smiled a catlike, smug smile. "Zahra will not always be here to protect you," she said. "Perhaps when she leaves I will ask for you to be my own personal slave. I am sure the Emir will grant my every wish most willingly." She laughed and tripped over to where Nabeela and the other two girls were waiting for her.

Angeline kept her head high. She forced a disdainful smile and a casual shrug but she could feel her insides shrivelling.

What *would* happen when Zahra left?

Chapter Fifteen

It was not something that she could talk to Zahra about. Nor could she speak to Stephen or Father Martin. It was a worm of worry that curled itself inside her head and that she alone would have to endure.

Then one morning Zahra emerged from the Emir's rooms beaming.

"Come, binty. You are to start working for the Emir with me this very day!"

Angeline followed her to her room, her hopes rising. Surely, if she worked well enough and pleased the Emir well enough he would heed her wishes and not Heba's.

But she will be a concubine and make herself dear to him, a small voice insisted. *You will still be naught but a slave.* She silenced the voice. Enough! Time to worry about that later. For now she would work as hard as she could.

But when they reached her room, Zahra turned to her.

"I have even better news, binty. I did not want to tell you until we were alone. There are even greater things in store for you—the Emir has chosen you to be a concubine!"

Angeline gasped.

"But I thought Heba . . . ?"

"So did she," Zahra said with a laugh. "But she did not take me into account in her plans." She looked as smug and as satisfied as had Heba. More so.

Suddenly all became clear.

"You planned this!" Angeline exclaimed. "That is why you insisted I come with you to the festivities on the Nile. Why you dressed me so beautifully, took such pains with me. You were showing me off to the Emir! You were planning that he should choose me as a concubine as well as a copyist! Was that so you could have your freedom all the sooner?"

"But of course," Zahra said. "This will serve me well, binty, and it will also serve you."

"I do not want this!" Angeline cried. "I cannot do it!"

Zahra's smile dimmed. She looked astonished.

"Why ever not? It is a great compliment. Your life here will be much improved. And when I leave, you will fill my place. You could not wish for better fortune."

"I *cannot!*" Angeline cried again.

Now Zahra frowned. "You must," she said. "No one refuses the Emir. It would be unthinkable. Besides, it is the best thing that could happen to you. You would prefer that he choose Heba?" she asked. "Do you not realize what misery that girl could make for you? I thought you would be grateful!"

Angeline brought herself under control with difficulty, but inside she was seething. How could she have ever trusted this woman? She had been betrayed—sold again—and there was nothing she could do about it.

"When?" She could hardly bring the word out.

"Tonight," Zahra answered. She seemed not to realize how angry Angeline was. "I will make you ready myself, with Samah's help." Her face softened. "Do not be afraid, binty. He is a kind man. He will treat you with courtesy. It is a great honour that he bestows upon you."

Angeline could not answer. She spent the rest of the day in a daze. She was to go to Father Martin that afternoon. When the time came, she was too distraught to think of a reasonable excuse not to.

"What ails you, child?" Father Martin asked her when she failed to answer a question for the third time.

"Nothing," she answered quickly. She looked over at Stephen, who was watching her with concern. What would he think when he found out?

She picked up her quill and drew a paper to her, but the writing on it blurred. To her horror, a tear dropped and the ink smeared. She rubbed at it with one hand, furtively wiping her eyes with the other.

Stephen was at her side in an instant.

"There *is* something amiss," he said. He laid his hand upon her shoulder and would have gazed into her face but she would not look up at him. Could not.

"It is nothing," she repeated. She took a deep breath and fought down the terror that was rising within her. Then she shook her head wildly and leaped to her feet, scattering quills, ink, and paper far and wide.

"Nothing!" she cried again. She shook off

Stephen's hand—met his eyes for one agonized moment, then turned and fled from the room. She heard him call after her but she did not stop.

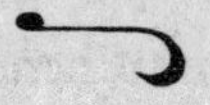

The terror rose and rose within her. Her mind churned wildly with one impossible plan after another, but the evening came and she knew finally that there was no escape. She gave up. She stood as frozen as a statue and let Zahra and Samah dress her and fuss over her. She stared out the window at the darkening sky. Pigeons flew, free and joyous as if taunting her.

Never again, they seemed to be saying. Never again will you walk with even the limited freedom of a slave. She had chafed at *those* bonds—how much greater were the bonds that lay ahead of her now?

She should have told Stephen. She should have bade him farewell, for surely, surely, she would never see him again. But she had not had the courage. Could not have borne seeing the light that shone in his eyes now when he greeted her die and his face grow hard. He would despise her. How could he not?

As a concubine her life would be restricted to the harem except for one or two outings a year such as she had accompanied Zahra on. She would never see Ibrahim and his family again. Would she even be allowed to see Father Martin? She did not know.

She tried not to think of the Emir. Of the night that lay ahead. Zahra dotted her special lotus flower perfume onto her neck and arms. The sweet, heavy smell of it sickened her. Samah fitted her feet into golden sandals. Then Zahra fastened a veil upon her hair and let it drop over her face.

"You will go veiled now, binty, when you are out of this room. As do I."

She made it sound as if it were an honour. To Angeline, as the gauzy cloth dropped in front of her eyes, it felt as if it were a shroud.

She followed Samah through the familiar passageways. This time she did not remain outside the Emir's room, but stepped through the door. This time it was she for whom Abd'al Haseeb waited. She, whom he rose to greet, hand outstretched.

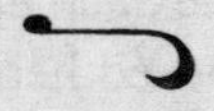

The very same servants who had brought her choice morsels of food and patted her on the head as if she were a pet dog when she had slept on the cushions outside the Emir's door treated her differently on the morning after she emerged from his room. They treated her with deference, as they had treated Zahra.

Now they deem me a person worthy of respect, Angeline thought bitterly.

She determined to go to the servants' hamman before she returned to Zahra. She had need of time to herself and, this early in the morning, no one else would be there. She resolutely kept her mind from thinking about the Emir. About what her life with him would be like from now on. She had nothing to fear from him, she had learned that. He was, as Zahra said, kind and respectful, but how could she live this way? In spite of herself, pictures of the years ahead of her unfolded themselves in her mind. Now, truly, she was trapped.

She entered the hamman and let her gown drop to the floor. Gratefully, she sank down into the cool water. She let her head fall back against the side of the bath and closed her eyes.

When she heard the Salat al-Fajr, the morning call to prayer, she roused herself. It was time to return to Zahra and begin the day's work. She could not bear the thought of facing the woman again, but she knew she must. Betrayed or not, she would have to keep learning from her if she ever wished to be free, and now she was more determined than ever to achieve liberty. She could not live this way for the rest of her life!

She walked up the steps out of the pool and dried herself with a cloth that hung nearby, then left the hamman and made her way to the staircase leading down to the kitchen. She would pick up Zahra's morning meal on her way. Then she paused. Would she continue to serve Zahra? Probably not. That, at least, was a blessing. She probably should not even have gone to the servants' hamman this morning. Would she go to the concubines' bath now? Would *she* have a servant or slave? It was the last thing she wished.

At the top of the staircase she heard a noise behind her. She turned. Anka and Heba, closely followed by Nabeela and Raful, stepped out of a connecting passageway and confronted her.

"Very grand you think yourself, don't you," Heba sneered. Her face was contorted with rage. She reached out and gave Angeline a push.

"Zahra's pet!" Anka jeered. She gave Angeline a prod as well.

Nabeela and Raful, encouraged by the other two, shoved her back a step.

"La'!" Angeline cried. *No!* "Leave me alone!"

Their only response was to encircle her and shove her harder, bumping her back and forth from one to another.

At that something seemed to break within her.

She could bear no more. She hit out with one hand and slapped Heba hard on the face. It was more of a blow than a slap. Heba gasped and put a hand to her cheek. Anka flushed scarlet.

"You dare to hit us, you swinish Franj?" she cried.

All four girls swarmed upon her. Angeline stepped back, trying to get away from them. Her foot caught on a loose corner of the rug beneath her feet and, before she could save herself, she felt herself falling down the stone staircase. Frantically, she reached out for something to stop her fall, but her hands closed on air. She was vaguely aware of someone screaming and realized it must be she. Then she lost consciousness.

When she regained her senses she was lying on her bed in Zahra's room. Faces peered down at her. Zahra and a man she could not recognize. What was a man doing in Zahra's room? she thought stupidly. She tried to move, but pain shot through her like a blazing knife. She fell back and swooned once more.

When she woke, the window of Zahra's room was dark. It must be night. Had she been unconscious for the whole day then? Again, she tried to sit up, but Zahra was beside her and she put a restraining hand on her shoulder.

"Be still, binty. Do not try to move," she said. "You have hurt your leg badly. The doctor has encased it in plaster but you will have to lie here until it heals." She cocked her head at Angeline. "The Emir's third wife, Nusaybah, sent her own physician to tend you when she heard what had happened. You are a surprising child—how did you ever come to meet her?"

Angeline could not summon strength enough to answer her.

"Never mind. You will tell me of that later. For now, you must rest."

Zahra laid a hand on Angeline's forehead. It felt cool and soft. She was trying to smile, but her face was drained of colour and her eyes were big with worry.

"What is wrong with my leg?" Angeline asked. The effort of speaking was almost too much for her.

"The bones are broken," Zahra answered.

"Bones?" Angeline asked. "More than one?"

Zahra caught her lip between her teeth, as if she had said more than she meant to.

"Yes," she answered reluctantly.

Angeline craned her head to look down at her leg. The effort made her dizzy and she had to grit her teeth to avoid being sick. Her leg was encased in a glistening, damp, hard white binding from her ankle to her thigh. She tried to move it but could not. The effort made her cry out, and she fought down another wave of nausea.

"Will it heal?" she asked in a whisper.

"Of course it will," Zahra answered quickly. Too quickly. "Of course it will."

"And if it doesn't?"

"It will," Zahra repeated. "Nusaybah's physician is the most skilled in Cairo."

Her words were meant to be reassuring, but her face gave the lie to them. Angeline sank back.

A cripple.

She was to be crippled for life.

Chapter Sixteen

"I thought you might like to start working again." Zahra pulled the low table over to the bed where Angeline lay. The book Angeline had been copying before the accident lay on it, with paper and ink waiting beside it.

Angeline drew herself up. It had been several days since her fall, but her leg still sent shafts of fire through her whenever she moved. She looked at the book. Her first thought was to refuse and lie back down. What was the use?

"It is only your leg that is broken, binty," Zahra said quietly. "There is nothing wrong with your hands—or your mind. Work will make the time pass more quickly."

Reluctantly, Angeline picked up the quill. The effort of writing exhausted her. She was too drained even to remain angry at Zahra. In spite of everything, however, she became immersed in the work. The book she was copying was a journal written by an "Arab-Syrian Gentleman." It told about his experiences during the time of the first crusades, almost a hundred years ago. She could not understand all of it, but what she could read was interesting enough to keep her mind off her own troubles. It certainly gave a different view of the crusades than what the priests at home had given. Not holy wars in this gentleman's opinion, just out and out invasions. It made her think.

The time did pass more quickly and she was surprised to hear the noon call to prayer. Aza came in to share their meal with them and hopped up onto Angeline's bed. Angeline suppressed a grimace as she was jolted, but managed to shift to make room for the child.

"Are you better yet?" Aza asked.

"Not yet," Angeline answered, but the question brought her back to herself and she had to stifle sudden tears.

"Soon she will be," Zahra said, coming

quickly to her side. "Now you must go with Samah and let Angeline rest."

Zahra was by Angeline's side nearly every moment of the day. She brought her food and waited on her as if she, not Angeline, were the servant. Angeline was grateful, but it only made her more desolate. She must be badly injured indeed for Zahra to take such care of her. And what about the Emir? Would he still want her as a concubine if she were crippled? She dared not ask.

One afternoon, while she was resting, Zahra woke her with a soft hand on her shoulder.

"Heba and the others are here. They ask if you will see them."

Anger surged through her. She never wanted to see any of them again as long as she lived.

"No," she replied.

"They have come to apologize," Zahra said. "They are truly sorry. They did not mean to cause such harm to you."

"I will not see them," Angeline repeated. She turned her face to the wall. This time she made no effort to staunch the tears that poured down her cheeks.

A few days later, on a morning when Zahra returned to the room after spending the night with the Emir, she went over to sit beside Angeline.

"Abd'al Haseeb has spoken to me about you," she said. Her face was solemn. "He is very distressed about your accident. He has told me to tell you that you are not to worry. Our faith commands us to care for those who are sick or ailing in any way. You will be taken care of no matter how badly you are injured. You may continue your work and take my place as copyist when I leave, but . . ." she stopped.

"But?" Angeline asked.

"But he has taken Heba as his new concubine."

"He does not want me anymore?"

"No. I am so sorry, binty."

Relief flooded through Angeline. She could continue to work, but she need not go again to the Emir! It was the first small bit of comfort she had been given. And surely now Heba would desist from tormenting her. Surely she had done enough.

"It means you will still be treated as a slave," Zahra said, "but you will be able to go to your priest as before."

"Will I be able to continue working for my freedom?" Angeline asked.

"Of course."

"And I will not be Heba's slave?"

"No. The Emir has promised me that. And, now that he has Heba as his new concubine and you will take my place as a copyist, he has told me that I am free to leave."

Angeline looked at her, surprised. So soon? Her heart sank. She was not ready for this. What would her life be like without Zahra to protect her? Despite Zahra's words of reassurance, Angeline felt a stab of fear and then, to her astonishment, regret. Suddenly, she realized how much she would miss the concubine and her little daughter.

Zahra must have seen the concern in her eyes.

"The Emir has given me my freedom, binty, but he has also given me permission to stay with you until you are recovered."

"To stay?" Angeline echoed stupidly. She knew how anxious Zahra was to leave, how keenly she looked forward to starting her new life. She could not believe Zahra would postpone that freedom just for her.

But Zahra nodded. "Yes," she answered.

"Why?" Angeline asked, incredulous. "Why would you do this for me?"

Zahra smiled. "Because I have grown fond of you, binty. You have my spirit."

Angeline let out a sigh. Perhaps there was a way, after all, that she could face the days ahead.

"Shukran, Setti," she said. Truly, she had misjudged Zahra. She pulled the table over to her and began to work.

Even so, the days dragged. It would be weeks before the plaster came off her leg, the doctor said. Her work kept Angeline's mind busy during the days, but at night she lay sleepless for hours at a time. She longed to see Stephen again, but she was afraid. What if he did not want to see her? He must know that she had lain with the Emir as his concubine. What did he think of her now?

Then, one morning, Zahra had an announcement.

"Your priest has asked to see you and permission has been granted," she told her. "He will come this afternoon."

Angeline's first thought was that finally she would have news of Stephen. But was Father Martin coming to condemn her?

When he was ushered in, however, he came quickly to her bedside and knelt beside her. In his face there was nothing but concern.

"How fare you, Angeline?" he asked. "We have worried so about you."

"I am not in so much pain now, Father. But—oh, Father, I have sinned. It was not of my own doing, I had no choice, but I have sinned. And now I do not know if I will walk again! The doctor will not be able to tell how well my leg has healed until they take this great plaster off me." Again, the tears overflowed.

How weak I have grown, Angeline thought. She swiped at her wet cheeks angrily and willed the weeping to stop.

"We will pray together, my child," Father Martin said. "You will make your confession. God will hear you."

The priest's low voice, praying in words that were old and familiar to her, went far to soothe her spirit. When he had finished she was able to look at him more closely and think, for the first time that day, of him.

"You look better," she said. "Last I saw you, you were so ill."

He flushed. "I allowed the Emir's doctor to treat me," he said shamefacedly. "Stephen would not cease pestering me until I agreed. A slight stomach ailment it was, no more. His medications have helped."

"How fares Stephen?" Angeline dared to ask then.

"As worried about you as I," Father Martin answered. "Perhaps even more so. But he is better, too. In spirit. He has made a friend."

Angeline looked at Father Martin sharply. He flushed an even brighter shade of red.

"A Copt," he said. "Named Ibrahim. Stephen said that you had introduced them." He tried to look disapproving, but did not quite manage it. "You did not tell me you were visiting a Coptic Christian church," he said.

"I thought you would not approve," Angeline said.

"Nor would I have. But I have done some thinking these past weeks. When Stephen told me of this friend I went with him to see for myself what this church was like." He stopped and looked down at the rosary he clasped in his hands. "I must confess I had a longing to be in a church again," he said quietly. "Even a Coptic church."

"And . . . ?" Angeline prompted him.

"And I found that our differences are not so great as I had imagined. I talked with Ibrahim's priest, and I have visited him often since. Perhaps I would be censured by others of my religion back in France for doing so, but I am not back in France, nor will I ever be. I am here now and will stay here until I die. I will find comfort where I can. I cannot believe that my God would blame me for that." He paused and looked at Angeline. "Nor can I believe that He would condemn you, Angeline, for what you were forced to do."

Now it was Angeline's turn to flush. She looked away, unable to meet his eyes.

What about Stephen? Would Stephen feel the same way?

Finally, the doctor decreed that it was time to remove the plaster. He came with sharp knives and cut it open. Zahra stood beside Angeline and held her hand. They both watched, hardly daring to breathe, as the cast fell off in pieces.

Angeline looked at her leg with horror. Could this withered, dead white thing possibly belong to her?

"Bend it," the doctor ordered.

Angeline looked to Zahra, too frightened to try.

"Go ahead, binty," Zahra said.

Angeline willed the knee to bend and was surprised to see it obey. She still could not believe this leg was part of her body.

The doctor smiled. "My work has been good," he said. "Now it is up to you. You must walk for a short time each day and strengthen it."

"*Can* I walk?" Angeline asked dubiously.

"There is no reason why not," he answered. "But," he added briskly, "you may limp. There is nothing to be done about that. Use a stick to support yourself." Then, smiling still, he left.

"Samah, fetch a good stout stick," Zahra ordered. Samah disappeared, then reappeared with a sturdy rod.

"I stole it from that old rascal, Kareem," she said with a grin.

"Now, binty," Zahra said, "you must get up."

"Not yet," Angeline protested. "It's too soon. Perhaps later?"

"Now," Zahra insisted. "We must begin sometime and now is as good as any other." She reached down and held Angeline as she sat up cautiously and lowered her legs to the floor.

"Lean on me and stand," Zahra ordered. "Use Samah's good stick to balance yourself."

"I can't . . ."

"You can."

Zahra put her arm around Angeline's shoulder. Angeline took a deep breath and put her weight onto her legs. Her injured leg buckled and she would have fallen had Zahra not been supporting her.

"I cannot do this," Angeline cried. To her shame, tears sprang to her eyes yet again. What a wretched mess she was!

"You can," Zahra insisted. "Try once more and then you can rest."

Angeline held Zahra's hand tightly, took another breath, and attempted once more to stand. Her injured leg shook, but it did not buckle.

"There!" Zahra exclaimed triumphantly. "You see? You *can* do it!"

She allowed Angeline to rest then, but each day she encouraged her to do more. Finally, with the help of Samah's stick, Angeline was able to walk about the room. But the doctor's fears were realized. She walked with a limping, hobbling gait.

Like an old beggar woman, Angeline thought bitterly.

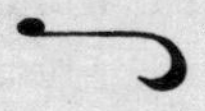

"Have you told Stephen that I am crippled?" she asked Father Martin the next time he was allowed to visit her.

"I have told him that you are up and walking and he is much relieved," the priest answered. "He is anxious to see you. When you can walk farther, Zeid has told us that you may resume your prayers and lessons with us."

"I cannot!" Angeline cried. Then she added quickly, "I will not be able to manage the stairs." But she knew that was not the truth. The real reason was that she could not face Stephen. Could not bear for him to see her crippled. Did not dare see contempt in his eyes for what she had done.

In the days that followed, she felt as if she were being torn in half. She wanted desperately to see Stephen, but she could not summon up the courage to do so, despite Father Martin's urgings. She steadfastly refused to begin their lessons again. Nor could she even contemplate a time when she might go back to visit Ibrahim, even if she could walk that far. She would not let herself think of him. Of Mariam. Of the family that had grown so dear to her. They would not want a concubine in their house.

"Are you saying that you never want to see Stephen again?" Father Martin demanded finally, exasperated. "That you no longer wish to learn to read and write?"

She would not answer him.

The Feast of Epiphany came and passed. The sounds of music and celebrations drifted in through Angeline's window and swirled around her, filling her mind with memories. This time last year she had gone with Zahra to take part in the festivities. She and Zahra had eaten together almost as equals. And when she had seen Zahra's delight at being outside the harem, she had pitied her. Never would *I* want to be a concubine, she had thought. If she had only known . . . She had been full of plans to introduce Stephen to Ibrahim. She had been full of hope. When she thought back on it now, she was surprised to find that she had even been happy.

Then came the day when she was forced to acknowledge a fear that she had been denying for weeks. At first she had tried to convince herself that it was because of her fall, but now she could delude herself no longer. She had not had her monthly flow for over three months.

She was with child.

Chapter Seventeen

Angeline lay awake all that night. She heard the muezzin's call to prayer at midnight and again at sunrise. She watched the blackness outside the window gradually lighten. She heard Zahra rise to pray, but she kept her eyes tightly closed and pretended to sleep. What would happen to her now? How could she care for a babe here? And without Zahra to help her—to protect her? Thoughts beat around in her mind like a wild bird trapped in a cage.

That day she performed her duties as if walking in her sleep. She dropped dishes and tripped over carpets. Still not entirely used to walking with her stick, she was clumsier than ever. Several times she didn't hear Zahra when she was called.

"What is the matter, binty?" Zahra finally demanded.

"Nothing!" Angeline answered.

"But there is. There must be. Never have I seen you so distracted. You must tell me what is wrong, binty."

"Nothing . . ." Angeline began again, but Zahra's concern and the worry in her face broke her resolve.

"I am with child!" she cried. She sank down onto a cushion and buried her face in her hands.

Zahra looked at her. "Are you certain, binty?" she asked.

"Yes," Angeline answered.

"But that is wonderful!"

Angeline looked up at Zahra, astounded.

"It is wonderful!" Zahra repeated. She sat down beside Angeline and took her hands in her own. "This means that when I leave you will not be so alone," she said. "I have worried about that, but now you will have a child to care for and love, as I have Aza. The Emir will provide for the child as he does for Aza, you need have no fear in that respect. The Emir cares for all his children. It is his duty, but it is also his pleasure to do so."

Her joy only deepened Angeline's despair. When Father Martin came the next morning, Angeline would not see him. How could she tell him that she was going to bring a child into the world? How could she tell Stephen? No possible hope, now, for Stephen's forgiveness.

During the next few days she tried to work, but could not. She blotched page after page until finally Zahra's patience was exhausted.

"The Emir is asking me why he is not seeing any work from you. He is growing dissatisfied," she said.

"I cannot work!" Angeline cried. "How can I work when I am in such torment?"

Zahra frowned at her. "You are in a torment of your own making, binty," she said. "There is no reason for it. And if you cannot work at the copying then you must go back to being a slave."

"But I *am* a slave," Angeline replied. She did not even try to keep the bitterness out of her voice.

"You will have to go back to doing a slave's duties instead of training to be a copyist. There will be no further talk of you working to obtain your freedom."

Angeline looked up, startled.

Zahra's face softened. "I only wish that which

will be best for you," she said, more gently. "You cannot change what has happened."

No, thought Angeline. I cannot change what has happened, but I would give my life to do so. It would have been better if I had died . . .

At that moment she felt the babe move within her for the first time. Amazed, she put a hand to her belly. She felt the faintest of flutters. Then—a kick. The tiniest of kicks, but definitely a kick! She felt it! And another. She looked at Zahra, her eyes wide.

Zahra laughed. "Is the babe kicking? Is it not amazing?"

And then it was as if all of her bitterness melted away. Her resolve, all of her courage, returned to her in one fierce, flooding, defensive wave. This was her child! And she knew without a doubt that she would do whatever was necessary to protect it.

She would heed Zahra's words. A slave's child, even if born free, had naught but a life of servitude to look forward to. Only if she worked for her own freedom would her child have any kind of chance here.

"You are right, Setti," she said. "And you are kind. More kind than I deserve, probably." She would tell Father Martin of the babe. She would face Stephen and tell him, too. Whatever happened, whatever they thought of her, she had a duty now to her child. It was of the babe that she must think.

She sat herself down at her table and drew a book toward her. With one hand still cradling her belly, she began to work. Her Arab-Syrian Gentleman had been about to go lion hunting when she had left off. She would see what happened to him next.

When Father Martin returned she greeted him with a calm smile.

"I'm ready to resume my lessons with you and Stephen, Father," she said. "May I begin again?"

"You may," he replied, "and I'm delighted to hear it. But it will just be you and me. Stephen is not here now."

"Not here?" Angeline repeated stupidly. She had never considered Stephen leaving. "What do you mean, Father? Where is he?" She suddenly felt sick. What if Stephen had been sent away? How could she have been so senseless, so stubborn, as not to have gone to him before?" Her carefully prepared composure deserted her entirely, but Father Martin's next words reassured her somewhat.

"He has gone with the Emir and Habib to Alexandria. The Emir has business there."

"How long will he be gone?"

"A few weeks. Perhaps a month," Father Martin replied.

Four weeks later, just as she was finishing up her lessons with Father Martin, there was a commotion at the door. She looked up to see Stephen whip back the tapestry that covered the opening and burst into the room. To Angeline's amazement, he was smiling broadly. His whole bearing had changed. He strode in confidently, eyes blazing. Here, again, was the boy whom she had seen inspire hundreds with his enthusiasm. She stared at him, speechless.

"Angeline!" Stephen cried. "How I have longed to see you! I have so much to tell you." He rushed forward, grasped her by the hand, and pulled her to her feet. Then, as he took in her swelling belly, his smile disappeared.

Angeline flushed. She waited for him to say something, but he stood, staring at her, dumbfounded. One long, ever-lasting moment she waited, then she thrust her chin into the air and, head held as high as she possibly could, she reached for her stick and pushed her way past him.

The following week she sent word to Father Martin that she would not be continuing her lessons with him. When Samah returned with a message from him urging her to reconsider,

Angeline ignored it. Then Samah came with a message from Stephen. He begged Angeline to meet him. Angeline ignored this message as well, and the next two that he sent. Finally Zahra intervened.

"You look dreadful, binty," she said. "You have not slept—I hear you tossing all night, and your work is sloppy. I have had to throw away the last three pages that you wrote. Go. See your friend Stephen and be done with it. You cannot go on in this manner."

There was no arguing with her. Angeline sent word that she would go back to Father Martin the following week. Zahra was right. She must be done with it. One last interview with Stephen and then she would not see him again. She would concentrate on her copying work for the Emir. Concentrate on working for her freedom, however long it took. This would be her life now. Her life with Stephen was over. Father Martin she would see. He had been kind and understanding about the child, although saddened that the babe would be born out of Christian wedlock. But even so was I born out of wedlock, Angeline thought. It is not such a dreadful thing. And I will be as good a mother to this child as my mother was to me. This child will know love from the moment it is born.

But, in spite of her resolve, when the time

came she approached the classroom with dread. She had to force herself to take one limping step after another. She leaned heavily on Samah's stick. And then, as she entered the room, the dread was replaced with anger. How dare Stephen judge her! She welcomed the anger, fed it. It would help her to be strong enough to do what had to be done. Say what had to be said.

Stephen was waiting for her. He rose as she entered and took a step toward her but she stood where she was, defiant.

"Angeline," Stephen said. "Forgive me. I did not know about the child! Father Martin had not time to tell me."

"It matters not," Angeline replied stiffly. "I am well. I can take care of myself. And my babe."

"It took me by surprise," Stephen protested. "I was so full of my own news . . . Come, sit with me."

Only then did Angeline realize that the priest was not in the room.

"Where is Father Martin?" she asked.

"I asked leave of him to let me speak to you alone," Stephen answered. "I have much to tell you."

"I think not," Angeline said. "You see what has happened to me. I am crippled and I will bear a child. We must go our separate ways now."

"But that is exactly what we must *not* do!" Stephen said. "You *must* hear what I have to say."

Angeline set her mouth firmly and armed herself against him. Pity would be all that he could offer and she could not, would not, accept it. She allowed him to guide her to the couch, however, and sank down onto it thankfully. She would not have him see how her knees were trembling, how weak she was.

"First of all," Stephen said, "I am a slave no longer. The Emir has given me my freedom."

"You are free!" Angeline exclaimed, startled out of her anger. "But how . . . ?"

"It is a long story. Listen, now." Stephen faced her and took her hand. Angeline sat, too stunned to object.

"When we went to Alexandria, Habib was given permission to explore the city as long as I was with him. On that first day we went to the suq but then, at the far end of it, we could see a pillar of stone rising tall into the sky. Habib immediately wanted to go and see it more closely. The pillar was set high on a hill, the ground around it rocky and uneven, full of trenches and great holes. There were the remains of some great building scattered around as well. Habib, as usual, was clambering over them and taking no care whatsoever. I was concerned about him, but there was no stopping his enthusiasm. An enthusiasm that was only encouraged when we came upon one smaller version of the strange figure that we saw by the great pyramids, and then another. Do you remember it, Angeline?"

Angeline nodded.

"Habib ran ahead of me, across a wide expanse of sand and bushes toward the ruins of what looked like old walls. I followed more slowly. Truth to tell, I was not paying much attention to him. I was lost in my own thoughts, wondering who had built these marvellous things—what people had lived here in ancient times. I was determined to ask Zeid. He knows an amazing amount about all sorts of unlikely things. Then I heard Habib cry out. I looked up and saw the ground open up beneath his feet. The sand poured down into the hole and before I could do anything, Habib disappeared through it as well.

"You can imagine, Angeline, how I felt! I ran to the gaping hole and stared down into it. A foul stink rose from it and I choked. I called Habib's name, but he did not answer. Then I panicked. I stretched full length on the ground and put my head into the opening. I could just see him. He was lying twisted and unmoving just below me. I began to lower myself carefully down to him, then the sand shifted again and I plunged into the darkness. I almost landed on Habib. I was stunned, but not knocked senseless. I knelt beside Habib and began to feel over his body for injuries. A shower of sand came down upon me. With it came stones. I caught Habib up and dragged him away from the opening just in time. A rain of small stones and then larger ones cascaded down onto the spot where he had lain. I covered him with my body and protected my head with my arms. When the deluge stopped, I raised my head and looked for the opening. It was no longer there, Angeline. Darkness surrounded us."

Stephen dropped Angeline's hand and leaped to his feet. He began to pace as he continued his story. Angeline stared up at him, too appalled to speak.

"We were trapped. For a moment I was frozen with fear. I could not think. I could see nothing, I dared not move a step. And the smell! It was the smell of death and it sickened me with every breath I took. Then I thought I detected a glimmer of light. I sat still, hardly daring to breathe, as if the slightest movement on my part would cause it to disappear. The light drew closer. It grew brighter. Finally I could make out the flame of a torch.

"I cried out. There was no answer but, dimly, I could see the figure of a man holding the brand.

He gestured to me to follow him. I picked Habib up and carried him.

"The light from the torch was barely enough to see where I was walking. We were in a narrow passageway. On either side of me I could see walls lined with alcoves. Each alcove was just the size of a man's coffin. In an instant I knew then what they were. They were tombs and the smell that was sickening me was, indeed, the smell of death. Some of the alcoves were sealed, but some were broken open and I could see bones within them."

A shudder of horror passed through Angeline.

"There was worse to come, Angeline," Stephen said. "I followed the man into a small chamber and here his torch illumined yet more work of nightmares on the walls surrounding me. Figures of men with the heads of beasts, one with a serpent's tail. In the light of the flame they seemed to move as we passed by. Even in the torchlight I could see that they were as brightly hued as if freshly painted. Blues, greens, scarlets the colour of blood. Habib was heavy in my arms. I could only pray that he would not waken in this terrible place.

"The man led me up a flight of steps. At the top there was a round chamber with a circular opening in the centre that might have been a well. I could almost believe I could hear water running through it far below. The man strode on ahead of me. We passed a room with a table of stone in the middle of it. Benches of stone sat around it and on it were broken bowls and cups. There were wine jars strewn over the floor.

"And then, at the top of yet another flight of stairs, a door with a bar across it. The man leaned his torch against the wall and put his shoulder to the bar. Groaning, as if it had not been moved for centuries, it gave way. He opened the door and gestured me through.

"I pitched through the opening, Angeline, holding Habib and shielding my eyes with one hand against the blinding light of day. I turned to thank the man but, even as I turned, the door clanged shut. I heard the bar fall back into place. At that moment Habib stirred in my arms."

"What did you then?" Angeline asked. They were the first words she had been able to utter.

"I took Habib back to the Emir and recounted to him what had happened. Habib only remembered falling through the hole and wakening to find that I had rescued him. When I described the place, the Emir knew immediately where we had been. We had fallen into the old catacombs, he told us. The burial place of ancient peoples long since gone. The entrance to them had been lost, he said, and no one went near them now. But of a man who lived down there, he knew nothing. That was impossible, he said."

Stephen stopped his pacing and threw himself down beside Angeline again.

"Truly, Angeline, I know not what happened to me in that place. The Emir says there could not have been a man there, but I saw him. He guided me through the tombs as if we were walking through hell itself. I could never have found my way out without his help. Only once did I glimpse his face, Angeline. It was a momentary glance, in the shadows of his torch, but in that instant I felt as if I had seen him before. A long time ago. On a hill where I tended my sheep."

"How could that be?" Angeline asked in a whisper.

"I know not," Stephen replied. "And the more I think on it, the more dimly do I remember what he looked like. But for a moment . . ." He stopped. There was a long silence. Then he shook himself and jumped to his feet again as if possessed with an energy that would not let him be still. He went on.

" 'Thrice now you have saved my son's life,' the Emir said to me. 'I owe you much,' he said. 'It is a debt that is difficult to pay. How do you reward someone for a child's life?' I had no answer.

" 'I will repay you in the only way that I know

how,' he said. 'I give you your freedom. You are free to go. To return to your home.'

"My mind reeled. I could not take in his words.'There is a Christian merchant ship in the harbour,' he said. 'You are free to go to it. To return to your home.' "

"But you did not?"

"I went down to the harbour. I made my way to the ruins of the great lighthouse that overlooks it. Do you remember seeing it when we arrived here, Angeline?"

She nodded.

"I stood there and I gazed out across the sea. To our own land. To our home. Then I turned my eyes to the harbour and I saw the ships moored there. The Christian ship must have been one of them. A thousand thoughts passed through my mind. Memories of my father, of my brother. How would they welcome me if I returned?

"But you, Angeline. Could I really leave you? After all we have been through together? I knew I could not. I turned my back on the harbour and returned here with the Emir."

"And then you saw me," Angeline said bitterly. "You saw what had befallen me. Perhaps it is not too late for you to change your mind."

"I do not wish to change my mind, Angeline," Stephen said. "I wish to stay here with you."

"But you are free. I am still a slave and will be for years to come. I bear a child that is not yours." She gestured toward the stick leaning against the cushions. "And I am crippled," she said.

"None of which changes anything. I want nothing more than to be with you, Angeline. I will wait as long as I must and when you are free, if you will have me, I shall wed you and love your child as if it were my own."

"Is it out of pity that you do this?" Angeline burst out. She struggled to her feet and would have fallen had not Stephen sprung to support her. "If so, I will not have it!"

"Was it pity that caused you to stay by me when the waters did not part in Marseilles?" he asked.

"No, of course not!" she protested.

"Then believe me, it is not pity that brought me back to you. I could not bear to be parted from you now. I want nothing more than to be with you for the rest of our lives."

He put his arms around her then and drew her to him.

"I have spoken with Ibrahim since I returned," he said. "He and his family are sorely distressed for you. They want only that you should come to them again as soon as you can. And more! Yousef says there would be a place for me as an apprentice with him. He could use a Franj who has a knowledge of Arabic as well."

Angeline started to speak, but Stephen laid a finger across her lips.

"Only tell me that you feel for me what I feel for you, Angeline, and I will wait for you," he said. "We will marry when we can. We can make a good life for ourselves here. I know not what happened to me in that place of death, but I do know that somehow I have found peace. I have regained my faith. I can pray again, Angeline! But it will last only if I can share it with you. Do you, Angeline, do you care for me as I care for you?"

He looked at her and she could see the pleading in his eyes. She knew then that he spoke truly.

"I do," she whispered. "I always have."

She dropped her head against his chest and let his warmth enfold her. She felt as if she had finally come home.

Angeline returned to Zahra. At first she could not speak, and then the words tumbled out without stopping.

"But it will be so long before I can earn my freedom," she finished.

"Perhaps not," Zahra said.

Angeline looked at her.

"When a slave bears her master's child, the child is born free—I have told you that already," Zahra said. "But what I did not mention, because I did not know then that it might be a possibility for you, was that sometimes, if the slave wishes it, the master will allow her to marry and will give her *her* freedom as well."

Angeline stared at Zahra, unwilling to allow the hope she felt rising within her to surface.

"The Emir . . . ?" she asked. "Would he do that for me?"

"He is fond of you," Zahra answered. "You can but ask him."

"I? I would have to ask him?"

"Yes, binty. You would."

"But I do not know if I could face him again," Angeline said. "I have not the courage!"

"You have the courage of a lion, binty. You can do it if you want to badly enough. Do you?"

"Oh, I do!" Angeline burst out.

"Then I will arrange it."

The next afternoon Zahra told her that the Emir would see her. Angeline made her way to his rooms. At the door, she fought down the fear that threatened to overwhelm her. She paused and drew a deep breath. Then she handed her stick to the servant who waited there. She would walk in to face Abd'al Haseeb on her own.

He was seated at his table when she came in.

"So," he said, "it is good to see you, my little Franj. How fare you now?"

"I am well, Maulaya," Angeline answered. She willed herself to look him full in the eye although her spirit quailed within her. Memories of the night she had spent with him rose unbidden to her mind. She could not block them out. Her face crimsoned. She saw him look at her belly and the fire that flamed in her face suffused her whole body. It took every bit of strength she could muster not to drop her eyes.

"I am sorry for what those girls did to you," he said.

"It was an accident."

"You bear my child. How feel you about that?"

Angeline was startled. She had not expected this question.

"I welcome it, Maulaya," she said defiantly. "I will love my babe. I love it already."

The Emir smiled. "And you wish to marry?" he asked.

"Na'am, Maulaya." *Yes, Master.*

"Stephen. He who saved my son and whom I have freed?"

"Yes, Master."

"You have suffered much in my house," the Emir said. He stood and came over to her. He cupped her chin in his hand.

"I would see you happy again," he said. "But if I give you your freedom and allow you to marry, will you work for me still? Zahra will leave us soon, now. Your work is good. I would not lose you, too."

"I would be honoured to work for you, Maulaya," Angeline said. A great lightness began to pour through her. She could hardly force the words out past it. She waited for what seemed a lifetime for the Emir's next words.

"Then so be it," he said. "I am sorry matters turned out this way but, perhaps, for you it is for the best. You know that in any case I will provide for the child. Go now. Make your plans. You are a free woman and you may wed when you wish."

He raised his hand in blessing.

"Assalama alaikum wa rahmatallah," he said. *Peace be on you and God's mercy.*

When Angeline returned Zahra was not in the room. She walked to the window and sank down on a pillow beside it. The sun was setting and the pigeons were flying home to roost. She could not believe what had happened. She was free. She would wed Stephen.

The first notes of the muezzin's call to prayer

rang out. She let them sink into her soul. Vespers would be ringing out over her own land. The land she would never see again. Were other crusades being planned there now? Would men once more go to battle over the Holy Land? She could not hope that to be true. People lived together in peace here—Muslims, Jews, and Christians. Could they not do the same in Jerusalem?

She placed a hand on her belly and felt the life stirring within, strong and urgent. There would be other babes as well. She could only pray that they would never know war. Would never know the horrors that she and Stephen had lived through.

Tomorrow she would tell Stephen what the Emir had granted them. Tomorrow they could make plans for the rest of their lives.

But for now, there was something she must do. She pulled her table over to her and took up her quill. She began to draw. Four pictures. One for each of the girls who had caused her so much misery. Heba, Anka, Nabeela, and Raful. The girls she had not been able to forgive but who, ultimately, had given her life back to her. She drew them dancing. Full of movement and grace. She drew them as beautifully and honestly as she could.

Historical Note

After they set sail from Marseilles, nothing further was heard of Stephen and his followers for eighteen years. Then, in 1230, one of the young priests who had accompanied Stephen arrived back in France. He told of the storm that wrecked two of the ships, and of the children being sold into slavery at Bougie, on the Algerian coast, and Alexandria, in Egypt. Some young people had also been taken to Baghdad. There, the priest had heard, eighteen of them were killed for refusing to abandon their faith and accept Islam.

The priests and children who were sold in Egypt, and who could read and write, were more fortunate. There was a great interest at the time amongst the princes of Egypt in learning Western languages, so these literate members of Stephen's ill-fated crusade found themselves being used as interpreters, teachers, and secretaries, and no attempt to convert them was made.

Slaves were treated well in the Muslim society of Egypt; most of the children sold there eventually made good lives for themselves. Of Stephen's fate, however, nothing is known. I have taken the liberty of imagining the end to his story.

KARLEEN BRADFORD

2004

Acknowledgements

I would like to thank:

My editors, Lynne Missen and Kathryn Cole, for their expertise and inspiration

My agents, David and Lynn Bennett and Marie Campbell, for their support and guidance

Jan Andrews and Rachna Gilmore for their infinite patience in reading draft after draft

Rukhsana Khan for her help with matters concerning Islam

and the Canada Council for the grant that enabled me to do the necessary research for this book in Egypt

Shukran

CHAPTER ONE

The next morning Stephen rose as the church bell announced Prime, the early morning prayers. Carefully, he stepped over Gil's snoring body. He snatched up another crust of barley bread and a round of cheese that was only slightly moldy, then he opened the door and stepped out. It was early April and the day was still fresh and heavy with dew. He followed the clucking of a hen and pulled back the branches of a bush to find a newly laid egg. A treasure! He cradled it, still warm, in his hand, then carefully put it in the pouch that dangled from the rope at his waist. He would make a fire when he reached the field and cook it. A feast, it would be, with the bread and cheese.

He opened the pen and hustled the sheep out. They were stupid with sleep and he had to throw clods of mud at them to get them moving. A dog. That was what he should have. A dog would be a great help. But his father had cuffed him even harder when he had suggested getting one.

"A dog!" he had cried. "Do you think us so rich that we could afford to feed such a beast? No, you wastrel. Tending the sheep is your job. Do not try to squirm out of it."

Stephen had known better than to argue. But still, a dog would have helped. He would gladly have shared his own food with it. Perhaps he would not daydream so much if he had a dog to keep him company, to talk to during the long hours of the day.

He shrugged. It was not to be.

Several boys his own age passed by him, hoes and scythes over their shoulders. They would be on their way to the fields to work but he knew better than to call out a greeting to them, nor did they acknowledge him. Such was his father's reputation for meanness, and his brother's for bullying and thieving, that Stephen had never had any friends in the village. The tallest of the boys turned back. He was a lout named Yves who had delighted in harassing Stephen ever since childhood.

"A chicken was missing from our henhouse this morning," he spat out. "And Pierre here saw your filthy brother hanging around our cottage after he left the tavern last night. You wouldn't be likely to be having chicken in your pot this evening, now would you?"

Stephen flushed but, before he could answer, the boy turned away. Stephen bit his lip until he tasted blood. The worst of it was that the accusation might be true. Not that he would have even a sniff of the bird if it were. Gil and his father would finish it off long before he returned and his father would never question where it came from, either. It had happened before.

He threw another clod of mud at the sheep, a little too hard. It hit the lead sheep, the bell-weather, on her flanks. She looked back over her shoulder and gave him a black look.

"My apologies, my maid," Stephen called out, then looked quickly after his tormentors. All he needed was for them to hear him apologizing to a sheep, but by great good fortune they were too far ahead by now.

* * *

He decided to take the sheep up to the high field this day. It was farther, and a steep climb, and the pasture was not as good, but this field inevitably drew him. Stories were told of a great battle that had taken place there between their own King Philip and the beast of England, King Richard, whom they called Lionheart. Once they had fought on the same side, those two great men, on one of the crusades that had failed to reclaim the holy city of Jerusalem for Christianity, but then, only a few years before Stephen had been born, they had fallen out and fought against each other in this very place. The grass was littered with helms that were battered beyond use, bent and twisted pieces of swords, broken lances, bits of rusted chain mail. And bones, too. Bones of horses. Bones of men. Stephen could almost imagine the scarlet flowers that bloomed in and around them to be drops of blood. He had often felt the presence of ghosts around him in that field.

As he climbed, the sun warmed him. The sheep followed the bellweather on the narrow trail with hardly any urging on Stephen's part. The bell on the ewe's neck rang out with each step the animal took. The air here was so clear that the sound was sharp and clean. Stephen's spirits began to lift. It was always so when he climbed to these heights. He turned to look back. The village below seemed so small. Smoke curled from chimneys, here and there a tiny figure moved—to the stream to fetch water, to the church to hear Mass. From this distance it looked peaceful and safe.

He turned away and drew a deep breath. The sky was bright blue with the hint of summer in it. Only a few clouds scudded by. Beneath his feet some herb released a sharp, pungent smell.

His mother would have known the name for that herb, he thought. On the rare occasions when Mattieu spoke of her, he nearly always told how knowledgeable she had been about herbs.

"The village women came to her for their remedies," he said. "There wasn't an illness she could not cure."

From his father's words and how he spoke Stephen could almost believe that his father had not had such a temper before his mother's death. Certainly it seemed as if the women of the village had no fear of him then. And Gil, of course, would have been just a babe. It was hard for Stephen to think of his loutish brother as a small child hanging onto his mother's skirts. Perhaps he had even been shy. Would the family have been a happy one if he had not taken his mother's life when he was born? The thought laid guilt heavy upon him.

His father's temper had driven the village

women away, however, and their daughters avoided Gil and looked at him with contempt. There was no place for Stephen's family in the village now. There was no place for him.

He shrugged again. Such thoughts only led to sadness. He pushed them away and took another deep breath. Then he stooped to pick a sprig of the herb and tuck it in the rope around his waist.

When he reached the field the sun was high. The sheep scattered and began grazing. Something caught his eye. He bent to pick up a fragment of a sword. Who had carried this, he wondered? What had been his fate?

Only last Sunday Father Martin had railed at the men in the congregation, accusing them of deserting God. Of forgetting about His holy city.

"The crusades must begin again!" he had cried. "Jerusalem is still lost to us!"

Stephen had sat, letting the priest's words sink into him, fill him. He would not have forgotten. He would not have deserted God. Fighting for God must be the greatest act of faith a man could do!

Now he closed his eyes and again, in his mind, the noise of battle rose around him.

And then a voice cut through his imaginings.

"Come here, Stephen," it said.